Born and raised in the Australian bush, **Miranda Lee** was boarding-school-educated, and briefly pursued a career in classical music before moving to Sydney and embracing the world of computers. Happily married, with three daughters, she began writing when family commitments kept her at home. She likes to create stories that are believable, modern, fast-paced and sexy. Her interests include meaty sagas, doing word puzzles, gambling and going to the movies.

Visit the Author Profile page
at millsandboon.co.uk for more titles.

THE MAGNATE'S TEMPESTUOUS MARRIAGE

BY
MIRANDA LEE

MILLS & BOON

HarperCollins

PUBLISHERS

Since 1817

First Published in Great Britain 2017
By Mills & Boon, an imprint of HarperCollins*Publishers*
1 London Bridge Street, London, SE1 9GF

© 2017 Miranda Lee

ISBN: 978-0-263-92425-1

Printed and bound in Spain
by CPI, Barcelona

PROLOGUE

SARAH SAT AT her desk, twiddling her thumbs, bored to tears. Thank God it was Friday. Only a couple of hours to go and the working week would have ended, as would her tedious stint in Contracts and Mergers. Sarah hadn't become a lawyer to spend her days filling out forms and asking people to sign on the dotted line. Anyone could do that. It didn't take four years of study, doing a law degree.

When she'd been offered a job at the prestigious legal firm of Goldstein & Evans, Sarah had imagined herself becoming the champion of the underdog, righting wrongs and representing innocent people in court. Instead, in the seven weeks since she'd joined the firm in January, she hadn't even come close to setting foot in a court. She'd spent one week in Conveyancing, two in Trustees and Wills and then two in the family law section, which had not been to her liking at all. Still, at least it had been more interesting than what she'd been doing this last fortnight.

Sarah was infinitely grateful that next week she would be moving on to the criminal and civil defence team, which was more her cup of tea. They had a pro bono section where some of the lawyers—usually the new ones, she gathered—were assigned to people who needed but could not afford legal representation. Sarah was looking forward to that.

Meanwhile, she rolled her eyes as they returned to her laptop where she'd been filling in time, doing some research on a client who was coming in to sign a sales contract at three o'clock. For a diamond mine, no less! His name was Scott McAllister and he was supposedly some hotshot mining magnate whom Bob—her current mentor—said she should have known. Apparently he'd been on the TV a lot lately, because of a nickel refinery that was going bust, whose threatened closing down would cost a lot of jobs. Sarah wasn't a great watcher of news programmes so she didn't have a clue who he was.

The Internet, however, had a reasonable amount of information on Scott McAllister. One of Australia's youngest mining magnates, he had his finger in a lot of mining pies, having interests in iron ore, gold and coal as well as nickel and aluminium. And now diamonds, she added to the list. Apparently, he'd got his start after his prospector father had died over a decade earlier, the son soon discovering that two of his parent's seemingly worthless purchases of land held hidden treasures. One had some decent-sized deposits of iron ore underneath which had originally looked like useless rock. The other was chock-full of brown coal.

Bingo! Good old Dad. Luck, it seemed to Sarah, had played a big part in this McAllister's success. Not according to Bob, however, who insisted their client was a very astute man, who had a history of buying rocks of his own and turning them into diamonds, for want of a better word.

'Several reports stated that the diamond mine he's buying today is all mined out,' Bob had told her earlier today. 'But a man like McAllister wouldn't be buying it if that were the case. Clearly, he knows something that the present owners don't know.'

He'd sounded full of admiration for the man. Sarah wasn't quick to admire any man. But she'd looked him up just the same out of sheer curiosity.

Clicking onto a different site, she encountered a photograph of him that didn't tell her much other than he was very tall and very well built. It had been snapped at a work site where all the men, including the owner, were wearing yellow safety vests and yellow hard hats. The caption underneath disclosed it was a recent photo, taken at the nickel refinery last month during a strike. It was impossible to see what McAllister really looked like as he was also wearing sunglasses. Amazing how much the eyes told you about a man's looks. What she could see of his face was large and tough-looking, with suntanned skin, a strong nose and a squared jaw that could have been carved out of granite. A frown on his high forehead gave him a thoughtful look, but the set of his mouth was hard and uncompromising. He was reputedly only thirty-five, but he looked older. Not married, she'd also read, and decided that wasn't surprising. He didn't look like the type of man many women would take to, despite his wealth.

Bob's phone started to ring. Muttering a swear word under his breath, he swept it up to his ear. Thirty seconds later he swore even harder.

'Sorry,' he apologised to her. 'But McAllister has arrived early and the other parties aren't here yet. Neither have I finished reading through this damned complicated contract. Look, could you do me a favour and go down and welcome him? Take him up to the boardroom on the next floor and get him a coffee, or a drink or whatever he might like. You're good at that sort of thing.'

Sarah had no doubt she was. She'd been doing nothing much but getting coffee for Bob and his cohort since she started in this section. Might as well have been a waitress as well as a clerk. But her mother had taught her good manners, and excellent social skills. So she just smiled and said it would be her pleasure.

He beamed back at her. 'You are such a good girl,' he said.

Sarah might have taken offence if Bob had been any less than the sixty-three years he was. She was twenty-five years old. Twenty-six this year. Hardly a girl!

Rising, she smoothed down her skirt and pushed her hair back from her face before making her way from the office and along the hallway to Reception, glad in a way to have something to do. And to be honest, she was quite curious about the man she was about to meet, curious to see what he looked like without those sunglasses.

She spied him straight away, sitting all alone on one of the black leather two-seaters that dotted the large reception area. Dressed in a dark grey business suit, a white shirt and a rather dreary navy tie, he was leaning back with his arms outstretched along the back of the couch, his right foot hooked up over his left knee. His shoes, she noted, were clean but far from new. Fashion, she realised, was not one of this man's long suits. Maybe mining magnates didn't care about such things.

Disappointingly, his eyes were closed, but she could see the rest of him more clearly. His hair was dark brown and cut very short on top, and even shorter at the sides; a very macho look, which suited him. His nose was bigger than she'd originally thought, but his face could handle it. His mouth was wide and his top lip on the thin, slightly cruel side. His bottom lip was fuller, though not full enough to soften his hard face.

Even before he opened his eyes, Sarah knew Scott McAllister wasn't a traditionally handsome man but there was something about him that she found perversely appealing. Odd, since she'd never been attracted to big macho-looking males, always finding them physically intimidating. She much preferred lean, elegantly handsome men who had more brains than brawn.

She stopped a metre short of his feet and cleared her throat. 'Mr McAllister?' she said, a sudden burst of nerves making her voice higher than she would have liked. Her drama teacher at school had once called her voice lilting. She found it a touch girlish, not a voice designed to make a great impact in court. But she was working on it.

His eyelids rose, and she finally saw them. His eyes…

An icy grey, with surprisingly long lashes. Not hard. But definitely on the cold side. Yet strangely hot at the same time. Hot and hungry. They took her in with one long sweeping glance, *all* of her, making her breath catch and her cheeks colour. Not a fierce blush but a blush all the same. How humiliating!

'That's me,' he drawled as he unfolded himself and stood up, towering over her own five feet eight. And she had heels on as well! Not high heels admittedly, but still…

Her neck craned as she gazed up at him, her mouth having gone annoyingly dry. Suppressing a groan, she surreptitiously licked her perversely dry lips and adopted what she hoped was still a sophisticated persona.

'The present owners of the mine aren't here yet,' she said with one of those coolly composed smiles she could summon on autocue. 'So Mr Katon sent me down to look after you till they arrive.'

He didn't return her smile. Just stared at her, his eyes like molten steel.

A returning heat started up deep inside her, melting her core and making her want to do and say the most outrageous things. The control she had to exert over herself was enormous.

'If you'll follow me, sir,' she suggested, still coolly polite on the surface.

'Sweetheart,' he said, a small smile now lurking at the corners of that cruel yet sexy mouth. 'I'd follow you into hell.'

Sarah's mouth dropped open, the realisation hitting her with a certainty that was as strong as it was seductive that she felt exactly the same way about him.

CHAPTER ONE

Sydney, fifteen months later...

SCOTT STOOD AT the window behind his desk, staring blindly out at the view. Not that there was much of a view. The office block that housed the head office of McAllister Mines stood in the southern end of Sydney's CBD, not down at the more picturesque harbour end of town. There was no soothing water to look at. No sparkling Opera House. No beautiful parks or gardens. Just traffic-clogged streets and rather boring buildings.

Not that anything would soothe Scott that Monday morning. Never in his life had he felt such emotional upheaval. He'd been distressed when his father had died. But death, Scott decided, was easier to cope with than betrayal. He still could hardly believe that Sarah would do this to him. They'd only been married a year, yesterday their first wedding anniversary. And whilst Scott harboured a degree of distrust in the female sex, Sarah had been different from the women responsible for his cynicism. *Very* different. That she would cheat on him seemed...incredible.

The text—with photos attached—had arrived on

his business phone last Friday afternoon, shortly after he'd finished meeting with a Singapore billionaire who was staying on the Gold Coast, and whom Scott hoped would help solve his current cash-flow problems. Fortunately, he'd been alone at the time, as his first reaction had been utter shock. Followed by total disbelief. Gradually, however, he was forced to accept the evidence before his eyes. The incriminating photos, after all, had been crystal-clear, all of them stamped with the time and the date when they'd been taken. At lunchtime that very day.

And then there had been the accompanying message.

Thought you might like to know what your wife is getting up to when you go away.

It had been signed, 'A friend'.

Hardly, Scott thought bitterly. More likely a business enemy of his, or a jealous female colleague of Sarah's. His wife was the sort of girl who would inspire jealousy in other women. *And* in her husband. Not that that meant Sarah was innocent. His father used to say that if something looked like a duck, waddled like a duck and quacked like a duck, then the odds were pretty high that it was a duck. It didn't take Scott long to accept that his wife was having an affair with the superbly dressed, very handsome bastard who featured in those damning photos.

Scott would never have thought himself capable of the kind of black jealousy—and almost uncontrollable fury—that had seen him abandon his PA, Cleo, on the Gold Coast to finish his business nego-

tiations for him, making the excuse that Sarah had
been taken ill, then flying straight home to confront
his adulterous spouse.

But he hadn't confronted her straight away, had he?

A measure of guilt—or was it shame?—curled in
his stomach at what he had done.

He'd meant to have it out with her immediately,
still harbouring some vain hope that there might be
a logical explanation to this nightmare. But when
he'd strode into their apartment that evening, she'd
literally thrown herself at him, seemingly overjoyed
by his cutting his business trip short to be with her.
Her kisses had been wildly passionate, more so than
usual. Whilst their sex life up till now had been more
than satisfactory, Sarah was not an aggressive partner.
She always left it up to him to make the first move; to
take the lead in bed matters. Not that night, however.
She'd been quite bold with her actions, touching him
intimately as she'd kissed him.

Guilt, he decided now in retrospect.

Perversely, after she'd fallen asleep that night, ex-
hausted from their sexual marathon, *he'd* been the
one who'd felt guilty. Crazy, really. Why should he
feel guilty? *She* was the guilty one. *She* was the adulterer, not him.

She'd blatantly lied to him about what she'd done
that day—telling him she'd been shopping at lunchtime for a fabulous anniversary present for him. But
he knew exactly what she'd been doing at lunchtime
that Friday.

He'd left her then and gone to his study where
he'd acted like the Neanderthal he felt like, drinking
himself into oblivion before passing out on the sofa.

Which was where she'd found him the next morning.

And where their final ugly confrontation had begun...

It hadn't been pretty, Scott still stunned by the accusations Sarah had thrown at him. And the names. In the end, she'd walked out on him. And she hadn't come back.

By Sunday night Scott was forced to accept that Sarah might never come back.

Something that should have pleased him no end, but, perversely, it hadn't. As much as he wasn't the type of man who would countenance having a wife he couldn't trust, Scott couldn't get past the niggling doubt that maybe he'd been wrong to jump to the conclusion he had. Maybe he'd made a terrible mistake.

A knock on his office door startled him out of his troubling thoughts. 'Yes?' he bit out as he turned away from the window.

Cleo came in somewhat tentatively, the look she gave him speaking volumes. There was worry in her dark eyes and concern on her face. Scott had given her a potted version of the truth when he'd arrived this morning, knowing that it would be impossible to keep lying to Cleo. She wasn't just his PA. After three years of working closely together she'd become his friend as well. She'd been more shocked than he was, if that were possible, declaring her disbelief openly.

'Sarah would never be unfaithful to you, Scott. That girl loves you to death!'

Yes, well, he'd always thought so too. But obviously, he was wrong. Cleo, as well.

Scott would have shown her the photos, if he still had them. But he'd given the phone in question to his head of security last Saturday afternoon to have the damned things investigated.

Showing Harvey the photos of his wife with another man had been mortifying to say the least, but he simply had to make sure the photos were genuine and discover who had sent them. Plus he wanted to find out everything he could about the man involved. Lord knew what he would do once he found out his identity.

The man in the photos was facially handsome but he wasn't as tall or as well built as Scott, his frame on the lean side. Elegant, though. And a snazzy dresser. Scott hated him with a passion.

'Harvey just rang to say he was on his way up,' Cleo said, interrupting his jealous train of thought. 'Do you want me to get you both some coffee?'

Scott had been waiting for Harvey to report back to him all morning, but now that the moment was here he wished he'd never started on this course of action. He should have made Sarah stay and talk to him; should have insisted on her explaining those photos. Though what explanation could there possibly be? She hadn't denied their veracity. Her outrage that morning had been directed at him, and what he'd done the night before. Okay, so he should have shown her the photos as soon as he arrived home but he hadn't. Naturally, he'd still been too angry with her the following morning to apologise for what she called his caveman mentality. Her attempts to put the blame on him had almost worked, too. After she'd stormed out of the apartment, he'd begun to think that maybe she was innocent.

Till he'd looked at the photos again.

Scott's teeth clenched down hard in his jaw after which he glanced up at his patient PA. 'No coffee right now, thank you, Cleo,' he told her, doing his best to sound normal and not like a man about to face a firing squad. 'Oh, and, Cleo…thanks for standing in for me last Friday. I don't know what I would do without you.'

Cleo shrugged. 'Afraid I didn't do you much good. The investor made it obvious that he didn't like dealing with a female, especially one who's under thirty. Still, if you want my opinion, you're better off without his money. I didn't like the look of him at all. He had shifty eyes.'

Scott smiled a wry smile. Cleo had the habit of judging people by their eyes. And strangely, she was usually right. She'd prevented him making errors in judgment several times. And she had liked Sarah, had thought her the loveliest, nicest girl. He supposed no one could always be right.

'I'll scratch him off as a potential partner, then,' he said.

'That would be my advice. Still, you'll need to find someone else quick smart, Scott, or you'll have to shut down the nickel refinery. Maybe the mine as well. You can't keep running both at a loss indefinitely.'

'Yes, I know that,' he bit out. 'Look, do some research and see who might be open to investment. Someone from Australia maybe. Ah, Harvey's here. Come in, Harvey.'

Cleo left them to it, Harvey's poker face revealing absolutely nothing as he walked in. Harvey was in his mid-fifties, a big burly man and totally bald, with a craggily handsome face, an uncompromising mouth and cold blue eyes. He'd spent twenty years on the police force and another ten as a private detective before he'd become Scott's head of security. His bouncer-like appearance made him an excellent bodyguard, a job he'd done for Scott on occasion. Being a successful mining magnate did have its hazards, especially when a mine had to be closed, even temporarily. Despite his blue-collar appearance—Harvey was wearing jeans and a black leather bomber jacket—Harvey was also an IT expert, an invaluable security tool in this day and age.

Scott shut his office door then waved Harvey to one of the two armchairs in front of his desk.

'So what have you found out?' he asked straight away, hiding his escalating tension behind a brusque tone.

Harvey's eyes carried the closest thing to compassion that Scott had ever seen in them.

His heart sank, his stomach swirling with sudden nausea. Slumping into his office chair, he scooped in a deep breath then let it out slowly. 'From the look on your face, I presume you haven't any good news to tell me.'

'No.'

A man of few words, was Harvey.

Scott gathered himself in readiness for the worst. 'Okay, shoot,' he said.

Harvey leant forward and placed Scott's phone on the desktop before settling back into the chair.

'First things first,' he said matter-of-factly. 'The phone used to send you those photos was a throwaway. Couldn't be traced.'

'I suspected that,' Scott said. 'Were they real, though? The photos?'

'Yes. They weren't doctored in any way.'

Scott swallowed the bile that rose in his throat. 'What about the dates and times they were taken?'

'Also real. I was able to confirm everything by checking the hotel's security vision. They have cameras set up everywhere.'

'And what hotel was it?'

'The Regency.'

Scott's gut tightened. The Regency was a five-star hotel that was a stone's throw from the building where Sarah worked. 'What else have you found out?' he asked, resigned to more bad news.

'I spoke to a member of the bar staff who was working last Friday at lunchtime. He remembered Sarah.'

Of course he did, Scott thought grimly. Any man who wasn't blind would remember Sarah. She was a stunning-looking girl with long creamy blonde hair, big blue eyes and a mouth that would tempt Saint Peter himself. Add to that a slender but shapely figure that was always housed in softly feminine clothes and you had a package that drew every man's eye— and kept it.

Scott had never forgotten the first moment he'd laid eyes on her. It had been just on fifteen months ago. He'd been in the process of buying a clapped-out diamond mine he'd had a hunch about and had arrived early for an appointment at Goldstein & Evans, a Sydney legal firm he always used for signing business contracts. Sarah had been sent to greet him, acting more like an accomplished hostess rather than the newly graduated lawyer that he'd soon found out that she was. Scott had fallen madly in love at first sight. She'd confessed to him one week later on their third dinner date that she'd been similarly smitten with him.

And he'd believed her. Three months later she'd become his wife. One year later, it looked as if she was about to become his ex-wife.

Scott cleared his throat. 'What else did the barman say?'

'He said they looked pretty cosy together. Sat off in a very private corner. Didn't drink much. Just talked. Then after about fifteen minutes, they upped and left.'

'Right,' Scott bit out. They both knew exactly where they'd gone. The photos had told the story. First, the man had gone to Reception and booked a room. Then they'd ridden up in the lift and gone into the room, not emerging till forty-five minutes later.

'On the plus side, the barman did say he'd never seen her in there before,' Harvey added.

Terrific. But there were other hotels in Sydney's CBD. Heaps of them.

'The guy looked familiar, though,' Harvey went on. 'Been there with some other woman on a few occasions. A brunette.'

'Did you find out who he was?'

'Yup. His name is Philip Leighton. Mid-thirties. A lawyer.'

'And he works for Goldstein & Evans.'

'Spot on. In the family law section. He specialises in divorces. Society divorces mainly. People with money. His own family is wealthy. His father's a senator. Word is Mr Leighton has his eye on going into politics himself. He's not married and doesn't have a permanent partner. Quite the ladies' man, according to a work colleague of his I spoke to this morning. "A silver-tongued charmer" was the way this chap described him.'

Scott tried to blank his mind out to where that silver tongue might have been, but it was impossible, a black cloud of jealousy descending to darken his mood further. He hated being taken for a fool. And Sarah had taken him for a fool. Her outrage last Saturday morning had all been a sham to deflect attention away from her own guilt. The plain truth was Sarah had allowed herself to be seduced by that smooth-looking bastard.

Maybe if you hadn't been going away on business so much lately, it wouldn't have happened...

God, now *he* was making excuses for her!

Scott sat up straighter in his chair before sending his head of security what he hoped was a composed look. 'Is there anything else you have to tell me about my wife's relationship with this Leighton fellow?'

'Only that she didn't go to him after she left you on Saturday. He owns a house on the North Shore, and there's no sign of her—or her car—at his address.'

Was he relieved at this news? He didn't feel relieved. His gut churned some more.

'She's probably gone to stay at Cory's,' Scott muttered. 'He's her best friend. Sarah met him at university.'

Scott didn't elaborate, mostly because he didn't know all that much about the circumstances behind his wife's close friendship with the young architect. It came to him suddenly that he didn't know all that much about his wife's past all round. She'd told him during their whirlwind courtship that her mother was dead and she was estranged from her father and her only sibling, an older brother. There'd been a bitter divorce when she was a teenager, with the brother siding with the father, despite the bastard being unfaithful to his wife. He'd never questioned her further about her past. He'd also never grilled Sarah over her friendship with Cory, mainly because he wasn't worried about Cory. He rather liked the fellow. And Cory liked him back.

He probably doesn't like me now, Scott thought. *Not after Sarah told him what I did last Friday night.* And she would have. She told Cory everything. They were like two teenagers sometimes, laughing and chatting to each other on the phone for hours. Scott would have liked to be a fly on the wall at Cory's place right at this moment. Though possibly he wouldn't find out anything. It was Monday, after all, and both of them would be at work.

Suddenly, Scott wanted Harvey gone so that he could make some enquiries of his own. He stood up and strode around his desk where he stretched out his hand.

'Thank you, Harvey. You have gone over and above. I am most grateful.' At least he now knew where he stood. Though he still didn't know everything. And it was eating away at him. Did Sarah love this man? Had she ever loved *him*? Scott could have sworn she did. But then, he could have sworn she would never have cheated on him.

And she had.

'My pleasure, boss,' Harvey replied, rising to take

Scott's hand. 'Sorry I wasn't able to bring you better news.'

'Like our one-time Prime Minister said, Harvey, life isn't meant to be easy.' Or love. Because he still loved his unfaithful wife. Lord knew why!

As soon as Harvey was out of earshot, Scott took out his personal phone and brought up the number for Sarah's workplace. When he found out she wasn't at work, having called in sick, he wasn't sure what to think. Sarah never took days off, going into work through thick and thin. She loved her job, especially since being stationed permanently in the firm's pro bono section, which helped people without the funds to pay for a lawyer. She'd worked on a variety of cases so far, including one of unfair dismissal plus several sexual discrimination cases, most of which she'd won. It certainly wasn't like her to take a day off work without good cause.

Scott frowned. Clearly, Sarah was still upset. But with him, or herself? Maybe she'd only been unfaithful the once. Maybe she regretted it as soon as she'd done it. Maybe that was what her behaviour last Friday night was all about, her trying to make it up to him for what she'd done.

Suddenly another truly appalling thought occurred to Scott. Maybe she'd run off with this Leighton fellow, taken off interstate or even overseas.

Scott's heart did a savage somersault, then stopped entirely. 'Is Mr Leighton in this morning?' he somehow managed to ask the receptionist, his voice gravelly.

'Yes, he is, sir. Do you wish to speak to him?'

Relief had Scott quickly pulling himself together.

'Not right now,' he said firmly. But he would. Soon. First, he needed to speak to Sarah. Depending on what she revealed, *then* he would be speaking to Leighton. Though he doubted it would be a civil conversation. Scott could feel his temper rising just thinking of that sleazebag who thought nothing of seducing another man's wife. There was no doubt in his mind that Leighton would have been the one to make the first move. Sarah simply wasn't the unfaithful type.

Or was she?

It was becoming clear to Scott that maybe he didn't know his wife at all!

Shaking his head, he brought up Sarah's number, expecting that it would be turned off as it had been all weekend. It wasn't, but it *was* engaged. Who was she talking to? Cory? Or her sleazebag lover? On top of that, where was she? Still at Cory's place, probably.

Scott didn't hesitate, knowing that he couldn't sit there in his office, stewing over things. It was time to face Sarah again, and to insist on knowing where he stood. Grabbing his suit jacket from the coat stand in the corner, he dragged it on then hurried out to where Cleo was sitting behind her desk, frowning at her computer screen.

'Have to go out, Cleo. Things to do. Cancel any appointments I have this afternoon and take the day off. You deserve it.'

Cleo glanced up and sighed. 'You're not going to do anything foolish, are you, Scott?'

'Not today. I did that just over a year ago.' When he'd married a girl he didn't really know, a girl who was an enigma in this day and age.

Because Sarah had been a virgin when he'd met her.

As he hurried down to the basement car park Scott began to wonder with some of his old, well-earned cynicism towards the opposite sex if she'd had a secret agenda in keeping her virginity so long. Now that he thought about it through less rose-coloured glasses, how she'd got through high school then university untouched, along with two years backpacking around the world, was beyond credibility. Unless she'd always wanted to marry money, and had seen her virginity as the perfect weapon to ensnare the right rich sucker. Namely him.

Scott had come across quite a few gold-digging females since he'd made it big in the mining world, but none of them had been virgins. Not even close.

He hadn't questioned Sarah's inexperience at the time; had accepted her explanation that she'd been wary of the opposite sex for a long time because of her cheating father. He'd also eagerly swallowed the added seductive reason that till he came along, she'd never met a man who'd made her really *want* to have sex with him.

Not that she'd used the word, *sex*, at the time. She'd said make love with. Naturally. Nothing crude about Sarah. She was the epitome of femininity, her large liquid blue eyes windows to a soul that seemed as pure as it was incapable of deception.

More fool him. They said love was blind. *Well, they were right*, he thought angrily as he jumped into his Mercedes and gunned the engine. But he wasn't blind now. And he wanted answers. Lots of them!

CHAPTER TWO

'ARE YOU SURE you don't need me to drive you over there, sweetie?' Cory said. 'You might need help to carry things. I can easily take the afternoon off work. We have flexible hours here.'

'Thanks for the offer, Cory, but I would rather do this by myself.'

'And you're quite sure Brutus won't be there?'

Sarah winced at the new nickname Cory had given Scott. Not that it wasn't appropriate. The man was a brute to do what he had last Friday night, all under the guise of passion. Her stomach curled at all that she had allowed, and enjoyed. That was the worst part. How much she had enjoyed Scott's ravishing of her entire body. Her face flamed at the memories of the humiliating noises she'd made, the way she'd pleaded with him not to stop.

When she'd found out the next morning that he'd acted out of jealousy and revenge, her shock had quickly changed to fury.

'You don't honestly think he wouldn't have gone to work, do you?' she said bitterly. 'Trust me when I say only an atomic bomb landing on him would keep Scott away from his precious office on a Monday morning.'

'From what you told me, last Saturday morning was a little like an atomic bomb going off.'

Sarah was not a girl who lost her temper easily. But when she did…

'I can't tell you how mad I was!'

'You don't have to, sweetie. I saw for myself when you arrived at my place. You were spitting chips. Till you started crying, that is. For a while there over the weekend, I thought I might need a life jacket.'

'Please don't try to make me laugh, Cory. That man has broken my heart. What he did was unforgivable.'

'Why? Because he acted like a lot of men might have acted? When I found out Felix was cheating on me I was hotter for him than ever.'

'But you didn't love Felix and I *wasn't* cheating on Scott!'

'But it looked like you were…'

Sarah groaned. 'I know. I know.'

'I think you should call Scott and explain why you were at that hotel with your lawyer friend. After all, from what you told me those photos were pretty damning.'

'And then what? Scott says sorry and we just go on to live happily ever after? I don't think so, Cory.'

'Ah, I forgot. You're a Scorpio. They never forgive or forget. By the way, has it crossed your mind to wonder who might have sent those photos in the first place?'

Sarah sighed. 'I've thought of little else all morning.'

'Someone you work with perhaps?'

'No one comes to mind.'

'It has to be someone who hates you. Or hates Scott, more likely.'

'It could be the same person who told Phil those rumours about Scott and Cleo,' Sarah speculated.

'You're absolutely right,' Cory said excitedly. 'I told you from the first that it had to be some kind of set-up. Otherwise how could he or she have been at the right place at the right time to take incriminating photos of you and Phil at that hotel? That's far too coincidental. I think it has to be someone you work with, Sarah, someone who saw you leave together that lunchtime and followed you.'

'But who?'

'Search me, sweetie. But I do know that if you let this destroy your marriage, then that person has won.'

'It's Scott who's destroyed our marriage,' Sarah bit out. 'The bottom line is he didn't truly love me, or trust me. He jumped to conclusions and didn't give me the chance to explain. He didn't care how I would feel because he doesn't really care about me. I can see now that I was only ever a trophy wife to him. Arm candy to be trotted out at social functions, with the added bonus of sex whenever he felt like it. When he's home, that is. Which has become less frequent during the last six months. I actually thought he'd cut his business trip short last Friday so that he could be with me on our anniversary weekend. What a fool I was in more ways than one.'

'Wow. You're still very angry with him, aren't you?'

'You can say that again. Look, I must go. The cleaners would have left by now and I want to be out of the apartment before Brutus gets home.'

'You're calling him Brutus now,' Cory pointed out drily.

'Yes, well, if the cap fits he should wear it.'

'You do realise that hate is the other side of love.'

'Oh, yes. I certainly do. Have to go, Cory. I'll see you tonight.'

'I'll bring home Chinese,' he offered. 'And some nice wine.'

'That would be lovely. Thank you.'

Tears pricked at Sarah's eyes as she hung up. Cory was a dear friend. And so kind. Whatever would she have done without him this last weekend? Sarah didn't have a lot of friends, her few girlfriends from high school having drifted away after she left school and went to university. The same thing happened after her poor mother died at the end of her first year of university. Unable to study—or grieve properly—Sarah had taken off to go backpacking around the world. By the time she returned to Sydney University two years later, her earlier student friends had also moved on. Her own fault, Sarah accepted, having not kept in touch via social media, depression dogging her footsteps for such a long time, especially during the first twelve months of her backpacking getaway. Europe remained a blur, nothing of the incredible sights she'd seen touching her soul or brightening her life. She'd gone from city to city in a fog.

It wasn't till she'd reached Asia that the fog had finally lifted. Maybe it was the truly warm, gentle people she'd met there. The children had been especially adorable and the twelve months she'd spent travelling through India and Thailand and Vietnam had banished her depression, plus her bitterness, showing

her that maybe it was still possible for her to over-
come her wariness where men were concerned and
find love. Maybe even get married and have children.
Though that had seemed a stretch at the time.

Still, by the time she'd come home to Sydney and
resumed her studies, she'd been way more open to at
least try to give the opposite sex a chance. Though
she'd still had no intention of leaping into bed with
anyone in a hurry. It had been an enormous stroke
of luck that during her first semester back at Sydney
University she had met Cory.

Sarah smiled wryly as she looked back on that
time in her life when she'd imagined Cory might just
be 'the one' to banish her wariness of the opposite
sex—and sex—for good. Not only was he fun to be
with, he was quite gorgeous to look at. Very sexy with
his blond hair, bedroom blue eyes and a buffed body.
Whilst she hadn't been mad for him—she hadn't
known what it was to be mad for a man back then—
she had found him attractive. He'd seemed attracted
to her as well. The 'life of the party' type, Cory had
insisted she join the university book club and movie
club with him and soon they'd been going out together. It wasn't till she'd finally decided to take the
big step and sleep with him that Cory had been forced
to come out and tell her he was gay. Apparently, up
till then he'd tried to deny it, even to himself, afraid
that his parents would reject him.

But they hadn't. After that, she and Cory had remained close friends, with Cory dating like-minded
men and Sarah eventually becoming resigned to
going to her grave still a virgin. Because no way
had she been going to go to bed with a man she didn't

truly love and trust; trust being the most important part. In her mind she'd pictured a straight version of Cory. Someone sexy and intelligent and kind.

Unfortunately, she'd never seemed to meet such a man, not even when she'd left university and secured a plum job at a large legal firm that had wall-to-wall men walking around their corridors, men who had showed they found her *very* attractive. But none of them had done anything for her, not even Phil, who was super handsome and super intelligent and really very nice. Too old, however, at thirty-five. Despite her lack of success so far, Sarah had kept dreaming that one day she would meet Mr Perfect, fall madly in love, get married and have at least two perfect children.

Scott McAllister's entry into her life had blown apart all Sarah's misconceptions over the kind of man she imagined falling madly in love with. For starters he looked even older than Phil, yet it turned out he was the same age. He *wasn't* traditionally handsome. Neither was he university educated. In fact he'd never even gone to high school, spending his teenage years travelling the outback with his prospector father. Despite that he was obviously intelligent, a self-made mining magnate with perhaps more money than manners; the strong silent type who didn't waste words, or time. Superbly fit, with the body of a champion boxer, Scott McAllister was a macho man in every way, bulldozing his way into her life with very little subtlety.

She'd never forgotten the moment they'd first met, Scott's normally icy grey eyes glittering with a raw animal lust as they'd travelled over her from top to toe. Her body had flamed in instant response. And from that moment, she'd been his. It had been just a matter of time. He'd asked her out to dinner within five minutes of meeting her. And she'd been unable to say anything but yes, her body consumed with desires which had been as corrupting as they'd been compelling. How she'd lasted three dinner dates before succumbing to Scott's constant requests to go home with him afterwards was a miracle.

Of course, he'd been stunned over her being a virgin. But not displeased. In fact, he'd seemed quite taken by the idea, confessing that he'd never been with a virgin before.

Soon, she hadn't been able to get enough of his big, strong body and his passionate but still considerate lovemaking. She'd adored how safe she always felt in his arms. How truly loved. Feeling truly loved was just as important to Sarah as the physical pleasure she experienced in bed with Scott.

Or so she'd believed, till last Friday night...

'Don't think about that night any more, Sarah,' she lectured herself aloud. 'You'll go mad if you do.'

Shaking herself violently, Sarah went in search of her handbag and car keys. Ten minutes later she was heading across the harbour bridge, making a list in her head of what she had to collect from the apartment. Work clothes, of course. She couldn't call in sick every day. Neither could she go in there wearing the jeans she'd worn all weekend, or one of Cory's track suits, which was what she was wearing today. She needed toiletries too, of course. And the rest of her make-up. After her argument with Scott last Saturday morning she'd bolted out of the apartment with nothing much. Her going-out clothes could wait till another day, she decided. Sarah couldn't see herself going out much in the near future.

But what if there wasn't another day? What if Scott threw her out and changed the locks? It was the sort of thing her husband might do. He was not a man who took kindly to being crossed, let alone betrayed. As much as she hated to admit it, those photos had made her look as if she were having an affair with Phil.

No, she would have to collect all of her things today whilst she had the chance.

Sarah took the exit that would lead her down to McMahon's Point, her attempts at a more pragmatic mood disappearing with the sight of the tall block of harbourside apartments that she'd called home for the last year. A happy home, she'd thought, despite Scott's many absences. She *did* understand that he'd been facing business difficulties during the last few months, with the mining industry not doing well, metal prices at an all-time low. His frequent business trips still irked her, however. But his returns were always extra joyful, last Friday night even more so after what she'd been through that day. She'd woken last Saturday morning with a delicious smile on her face.

Of course, at the time, she'd still been ignorant of the true reason behind Scott's insatiable sexual appetite. And whilst the memory of some of his demands was slightly shocking, she'd also been secretly thrilled that at last she'd taken a less passive role in their sex life. On top of that, if she was brutally honest, she'd found her husband's highly erotic lovemaking wildly exciting and extremely satisfying, her many orgasms addictively powerful. So she'd dressed and gone in search of Scott the next morning, already turned on by the thought that they would have the whole weekend together.

She hadn't been turned on for long...

Sarah groaned, annoyed with herself for revisiting that painful encounter one more self-destructive time.

'What a bastard,' she muttered angrily as she drove down the ramp that led to the underground car park, stopping at the bottom to swipe her key card through the machine so that the security gate would rise. It was annoyingly slow, but at last she could drive through. Despite telling Cory confidently that Scott would be at work, she was still relieved to see that his car space was empty. She parked her red hatchback into her own allotted spot, locked it up then hurried over to the bank of lifts that would carry her up to the luxury high-rise apartment that Scott had bought a week before their wedding. Clearly, he'd wanted to impress his new bride. And he had.

It wasn't the penthouse. But it was only one floor down from the top and was simply huge, its wide wraparound balconies having views to die for. The plate-glass window in the main living room formed a perfect frame for the Sydney Harbour Bridge, with the Opera House underneath it in the distance. The same view applied to the floor-to-ceiling windows in the master bedroom. At night, it all looked magnificent.

There were two guest bedrooms aside from the master suite, each with their own en-suite bathroom. Add to this two formal receptions rooms, a home theatre, another powder room, a gym and a kitchen that was large enough to satisfy the caterers Sarah employed whenever they had a dinner party. Which up till now was at least once a month. Sarah could cook but cooking several courses for a large number of guests—their dinner table seated twelve—and trying to play hostess at the same time was beyond her.

After letting herself into the apartment Sarah stood in the spacious marble-floored foyer for a long moment, remembering how impressed she'd been when she'd first seen this place. Despite not having been brought up poor—Sarah came from a middle-class upbringing—she'd been overawed by the size of the rooms, the expensive fittings, the elegant imported furniture. She hadn't wanted to change a thing.

Sarah made her way down the carpeted hallway to the master suite. As she entered what had once been her favourite area in the house Sarah kept her eyes averted from the neatly made king-sized bed, trying desperately not to think of how it had looked last Saturday morning with its tangled oil-stained sheets, not to mention the long blue chiffon scarf that had been draped haphazardly over the black lacquered bed-head. But despite her best efforts, Sarah *did* think about it, her mouth drying at the memory of how turned on she'd been by Scott binding her wrists like that; how he'd poured body lotion all over her and proceeded to show her exactly how much he knew about a woman's secret fantasies. When he'd flipped her over and poured more lotion over her entire back, she hadn't protested. Just pleaded for him not to stop.

And he hadn't…

Oh, God.

Must not cry over last Friday night any more, she told herself sternly. *Just get all your things and go!*

Sarah hurried on across the thick cream carpet and into her walk-in wardrobe, where she pulled down the two large cases that they'd taken on honeymoon to Hawaii. She'd been happy then. Very happy. Scott had seemed happy, too.

Maybe that had all been an illusion. Maybe he'd always been a bit bored with her in bed. Sarah imagined most rich men eventually got bored with their trophy wives, which was why they traded them in for newer models a lot, or took mistresses, women who did even more kinky things than what she'd done with Scott last Friday night. Maybe those rumours about Scott and Cleo were right after all.

No—*no*. She refused to believe that. She hadn't really believed it then and she didn't believe it now!

Well, if you didn't believe it, why did you rush into the hotel bathroom and throw up when the investigator said there was not a shred of evidence of Scott and Cleo having an affair?

The truth was, at the back of her mind, where old tapes from the past were stored, she *had* believed it. Of course she had. She was programmed to believe that most husbands were cheaters, and their silly wives forgave them much too often. It haunted Sarah to think what she would have done if the investigator had said the opposite. That yes, Scott was having an affair with Cleo. Would she have confronted him? Would she have left him? Was she actually leaving Scott *now*?

Perversely, the question of her forgiving him would probably never arise. Clearly, her husband believed she'd been unfaithful. More than likely, he would want a divorce. If there was one thing Sarah knew about Scott it was his black-and-white thinking. It was both his strength, and his weakness. Whilst she'd always admired his straight-down-the-line character, plus his total adherence to honesty and integrity, Scott could be slightly one-eyed over things. There was no grey in his thinking. Forgiveness would not come easily to Scott, not if he thought he'd been wronged. And he believed she'd wronged him.

Pushing aside this distressing train of thought, Sarah turned to begin taking some clothes off their hangers when she suddenly caught sight of herself in the full-length mirror that hung on the back wall of the walk-in wardrobe. Dear God, but she looked a fright. Her hair was awful, having not been washed properly in days. The need to recondition her straw-like locks with her own lovely products suddenly became a necessity. It wasn't as though Scott was going to come home unexpectedly and catch her, naked, in the shower. She had plenty of time to be out of here before he left his precious office.

But she still hurried, wanting to be out of the place as soon as possible.

CHAPTER THREE

WHEN SCOTT DROVE into the underground car park and saw Sarah's car parked in its allotted space, the frustration he'd been feeling at not finding her at Cory's house revved up a notch. She hadn't been sick at all, had she? She'd snuck home here whilst she believed he was at work, no doubt to collect her things, plus possibly anything else she fancied. He'd heard of such things happening to other men who'd come home to find their houses stripped clean.

This furious thought stayed with him during his ride up in the lift, his angry mood lessening once he let himself into the apartment and discovered that nothing was missing. The artwork was still on the walls and all the expensive knick-knacks still there.

When he called out to Sarah, however, she didn't answer, leaving him with the sudden far more awful thought that maybe she'd brought her car back—it had been a Christmas present from him—and just left it, then taken a taxi off to Lord knew where. The realisation that Sarah might have done such a thing, that she was leaving him permanently, and that he would never have the opportunity to find out the truth, made him feel sick to the stomach.

It was then that he heard the faint sound of water running somewhere. Recognising the sound, Scott dashed down the hallway to their bedroom, where he noted that the bathroom door was shut. Clearly, Sarah was having a shower. Scott could not deny the relief that flooded him. But there were some other confusing emotions too. Surely he wasn't hoping she'd come home seeking a reconciliation? Surely she didn't expect him to *forgive* her?

Glancing to the left of the bathroom door, he saw that their walk-in wardrobe door was open. Scott marched over to stand in the doorway, his hands curling into fists as he stared down at the two open cases on the floor, his teeth clenching down just as hard. Okay, so she wasn't looking for a reconciliation, then. Good. All Scott wanted—or so he told himself—was an explanation of her actions.

It had niggled him all over the weekend that he'd been neglecting Sarah lately, leaving her alone way too much, not giving her the kind of attention that she'd obviously been secretly craving. Last Friday night had shown him that, at least. She'd been a different woman in his arms that night. Wild. Wanton. Bold. The kind of woman another man would do anything to get, and whom a husband would never be able to forget.

Scott groaned at the possibility that Sarah might not have been thinking of him when he'd been inside her last Friday night. She might have been thinking of the man she'd been with that lunchtime, whom she'd probably been with every time he went away on business.

The sudden silence from the bathroom coincided with his mood turning very dark indeed. Scott threw off his suit jacket and tie, flicked open the top button of his shirt before kicking off his shoes then stretching out on top of the bed. His stomach churned as he waited for his unfaithful wife to emerge, but his mind remained hard, and cold.

Sarah dried herself quickly, wrapping her wet hair in a towel before grabbing the long pink silk robe that she kept on a hook on the back of the bathroom door. Not an overly sexy garment, it was nevertheless pretty and very comfy with three-quarter-length sleeves in the kimono style. No way was she going to leave it behind. Pulling it on over her flushed nakedness, she tied the sash loosely around her waist before tossing the towel aside then drying her hair properly with her hair dryer, which was much more powerful and efficient than Cory's. *With a much better result*, she thought as she ran her fingers through her long straight silky locks before opening the bathroom door.

The unexpected sight of Scott lying on top of the bed brought a gasp of alarm to her lips. Despite his nonchalant pose—his hands were linked behind his head and his ankles were crossed—there was nothing nonchalant in his chilly grey gaze.

'I gather you're not staying, then,' he drawled, his voice as cold as his eyes.

Sarah could not find her tongue, fear drying her mouth and making her heart pound behind her ribs. She'd never been afraid of Scott before but she was at that moment.

'No,' she croaked out at last. 'I…I just came to get my clothes.'

Scott uncrossed his ankles then sat up abruptly.

'There's no need to sound so petrified, Sarah. I would never hurt you. Surely you must know that.'

'You hurt me last Friday night,' she threw at him.

'Now you know that's not true,' he ground out, standing up and towering over her. 'You enjoyed every moment of what we did last Friday night. Please don't add hypocrisy to your adultery.'

Her hand whipped up to slap him but he grabbed it before she could make contact with his face.

'Come now, Sarah,' he said. 'Let's try to act like adults here, shall we?'

For a long moment she thought he was going to pull her against him. The intent was in his glittering grey eyes. Her already racing heartbeat accelerated further. When he released her, she could not decide if she was relieved or disappointed.

A rueful smile twisted his mouth.

'I suggest you go put some more clothes on and we adjourn to somewhere less…dangerous. I find myself unable to focus with you nearly naked like that. All I can think of at this moment is how much I still want you, despite everything.'

Sarah's mouth dropped open at his startling admission. Even more startling was the fact that she wanted him just as much. How perverse was that?

It rattled her, this irrational but powerful urge she had to close the space between them, to reach up and kiss that hard, angry mouth of his.

His eyes narrowed on hers, perhaps glimpsing the crazy jolt of desire in their depths. For suddenly, his hands reached out to grab her shoulders, dragging her against him as his head swooped.

She could have fought him; could have been the

ultimate hypocrite. But she didn't, moaning under his quite brutal kiss, melting against his big strong body, her lips and her hips betraying her own frantic desire.

Insane. All of it. Sarah knew he still thought she'd been unfaithful to him. But right at this moment she didn't care what he thought. All she cared about was the here and now. And the here and now was turning her on to a degree that surpassed even last Friday night. She kissed him back with a quite savage need, telling him without words that she was still his, no matter what he believed.

When he wrenched his mouth away, she groaned in protest, staring up at him with wide glazed eyes.

'God, Sarah,' he ground out, then kissed her again, obliterating every sensible thought with the wildness of his passion. His mouth stayed glued to hers whilst he stripped off her robe, tossing it aside with careless abandon. By then she was trembling violently, but not from cold. A large lock of hair had fallen across her face, and eyes. She stared through the strands up into his lust-filled face. It thrilled her, this knowledge. She was already lost to the mindless world he'd created last Friday night; a world of excitingly erotic pleasure, which didn't seem to possess a conscience, only a craving for constant satisfaction.

His hands slowly scooped her hair back from her face, bundling it into a tight bunch at the nape of her neck as he pulled her head back, his captive hold doing wicked things to her traitorous body. He glared down at her, his face flushed, his breathing ragged.

'Don't go thinking this means I forgive you,' he threw at her.

'I've done nothing for you to forgive,' she managed

to say. But he only laughed, then kissed her again, kissed her and touched her till she was beyond protest, let alone wordy explanations. When he scooped her up and dumped her sideways across the silvery-grey quilt, she just lay there, quivering with need whilst he hurriedly undressed. And then he was on top of her, and inside her, and she was making those animal noises again, holding him tight as she opened her legs wide and wrapped them high around his back. She moved with him, moaning his name and reaching for that moment when her flesh would shatter around his. Her climax came with a rush, making her cry out, wracking her body with wave after wave of pleasure. It was brilliant. Glorious. She gasped with the electric pleasure of it all.

But the moment the tsunami of ecstasy began to wane, common sense blasted back into her brain, bringing with it the crushing reality of what she had just done.

'Oh, God,' she groaned, her tongue giving voice to her acute dismay. How could she have let him do that, believing what he still believed? How could she have enjoyed it, knowing this? At least last Friday night, she hadn't known about those photos, or what Scott had been thinking.

Her face crumpled as she agonised over what he was thinking now. Possibly that she was the worst person that had ever lived.

His face betrayed a momentary confusion before his eyes grew cold once more. He withdrew abruptly, not looking down at her as he stood up and dressed. After that, he picked up her robe, his gaze scornful as he tossed it over her outspread nakedness.

'I'm going into the kitchen to make coffee,' he grated out. 'Join me there when you're decent. We need to talk.'

Sarah squeezed her eyes tightly shut as she gripped the robe with both hands, already regretting everything, the heat of the moment fast becoming a distant memory. What on earth had possessed her? She couldn't make sense of it. It wasn't love that had propelled her into Scott's arms just now. It had been something more basic than that. Something primal. Something that would not be denied. Was it just lust, or a cavewoman instinct that demanded she lay claim to her man in the way women had been doing since time began?

That last explanation made some kind of sense, Sarah conceded as she put her robe back on and made her way reluctantly to the kitchen. But she didn't like either thought. Because both made her vulnerable to Scott. He had to be made to understand that she could not stay with a husband who didn't believe what she was about to tell him. She didn't want his forgiveness. She wanted his trust!

Sarah swallowed at the sight of her bare-chested husband busying himself in the kitchen. Lord, but he was a superbly built man, muscles rippling down his back, his arms, his chest. At the beginning of their relationship, she'd found his size somewhat intimidating, till he showed her just how gentle and tender he could be. After that she'd felt supremely safe in his arms. Not so any more. He no longer inspired that safe, secure feeling in her. Instead, when she looked at him, her whole insides quivered with a fear that was dangerously exciting. *He* was dangerously exciting. She wondered if this was what her poor mother had felt for her serial cheater of a husband. Sarah could see now that desire could make a woman weak. Weaker than love, in a way. It was a horrifying concept and one that she vowed to fight.

Such thinking forced her to ignore the stupid feelings that kept fluttering in her stomach. 'Why aren't you at work?' she asked brusquely as she levered herself up on one of the breakfast bar stools.

He turned and carried two mugs of steaming black coffee over to the counter.

'I couldn't work so I went looking for you,' he said. 'You weren't at Cory's so I came home.'

Sarah refused to feel flattered by his leaving his precious office to search for her. 'You could have called me.'

He made a scoffing sound. 'Don't you think I tried? You had your phone turned off all weekend. Then, today, when I tried again, it was engaged.'

She dropped her eyes to the coffee. 'I was probably talking to Cory.'

'Not Philip Leighton?'

Her head jerked up, her eyes widening.

'Don't play the innocent with me, Sarah. I know who the man in those photos is.'

Any confusion Sarah was suffering from suddenly changed to outrage. 'My God, you had those photographs investigated, didn't you?'

'What on earth did you expect?' Scott slammed back at her. '*You* wouldn't tell me anything. You refused to offer any explanation.'

'I'd have told you everything if you'd shown me those photos when you first arrived home. But you didn't. You had to have your pound of flesh first, didn't you?'

'Perhaps I was distracted by the passion of your greeting,' he said with cold anger in his eyes. 'And the quality of your lies.'

'My *lies*?' Sarah was genuinely thrown. 'What lies?'

'You said you'd gone out at lunchtime last Friday and bought me a special anniversary present,' he elaborated in rock-hard tones. 'I knew for a fact that you were actually in a bar, then up in a hotel room with another man.'

Her cheeks reddened with anger. 'I *did* buy you an anniversary present,' she insisted heatedly. 'In a boutique on my way out of the hotel where I wasn't doing anything to be ashamed of. I can show it to you if you like.'

'It's a little late for that, don't you think? Unless I'm very much mistaken, we're headed for the divorce court. I'm just grateful that we decided to put off having children for a couple of years. Thank God for the pill, is all I can say.'

Sarah's whole world stopped with his mentioning the pill; she couldn't remember the last time she had taken it. Had it been last week, last month? The blood drained from her face at the thought of the possible consequences of her naivety and she groaned.

'What is it?' Scott said as he glared at her. 'What's wrong?'

CHAPTER FOUR

As Sarah faced the unfaceable, the blood continued to drain from her head, which had been in a total fog since all this started. But it wasn't in a fog now. It was in shock.

She'd fainted a couple of times in her life before. Neither time had been pleasant. But she remembered how she'd felt just before it happened. The clamminess. The sense that everything was tipping out of kilter. This time she recognised the symptoms before disaster struck, slipping off the stool to sit on the tiled floor with her head dropping down between her knees.

'What in hell are you doing?' she heard Scott ask in an alarmed voice. 'Are you ill?' he added, coming round to hunker down next to her. 'Should I call an ambulance?'

'No,' was all she could manage. It was just shock and, yes, a lack of food perhaps. She hadn't had any breakfast. Or lunch for that matter, Cory having gone to work this morning before she got up. He'd fussed over her yesterday, forcing her to eat and drink something. With him gone she'd neglected herself.

'I'll be okay in a minute,' she added weakly at

last. 'Just feeling a bit faint. If you want to help then make me some toast. And put plenty of honey on it.'

'Toast,' he repeated, sounding totally flummoxed. But he stood up and his trouser legs disappeared so Sarah assumed he was doing as asked. Finally, she felt well enough to get up, but her legs were still shaky as she climbed back on the stool and reached for her coffee, grasping the mug with shaky hands. She'd begun to shake inside as well, still not having come to terms with what she'd realised a little while ago. It was said that fate was cruel. But it wasn't fate. It was her own stupid fault.

Sarah smothered a groan, her stomach contracting at the thought that a child might have been conceived after last Friday night. Her stomach contracted with horror at the thought. A baby should be born out of acts of love, not acts of black jealousy. She could also have conceived today, which wasn't much better. But better than last Friday, she supposed. She'd sort of known what she'd been doing just now.

Sarah shook her head in denial of this last thought. She hadn't known what she was doing at all, had she? Not really. She'd been putty in Scott's hands.

Her eyes went to those hands as he spread the toast with butter first. They were large hands. Large and strong, with calluses on their palms from where he'd done hard physical work for many years. He hadn't always been a businessman in a suit.

'Feeling better?' Scott asked as he placed the toast in front of her.

'A little. Thank you.' Avoiding his questioning eyes, she took a few bites of toast, swallowing them down with some coffee.

Thirty seconds passed before he spoke again. 'It's time you told me exactly what happened at that hotel last Friday, Sarah. And I want the truth.'

Sarah placed the mug back down on the white stone counter, took a deep gathering breath then glanced up at his large and uncompromising face.

'The truth,' she repeated, sounding calmer than she felt. For Sarah wasn't at all confident that he would believe her. He might think she was making it all up. Still, if that was the case, then she could suggest he speak to Phil. Phil would back her up.

Half an hour ago, she would have told him to stick his demand for the truth, but things were different now. The possibility that she might be having Scott's baby had changed everything.

Sarah gulped, then started. 'I went there with Phil to meet a private investigator who had some information about you.'

'Me?'

'Yes, you. Phil approached me that morning in the staff room and told me he had it on good authority that you were having an affair with your PA, Cleo.'

'What? That's ridiculous and you know it!'

Sarah wasn't going to be put off by Scott's bluster. 'Is it? Cleo's an attractive woman. On top of that she's a widow.'

An angry colour slanted across Scott's high cheekbones. 'I am *not* having an affair with Cleo. As for her being a widow, I'll have you know that Cleo is still very much in love with her dead husband. She would never even look at another man, let alone sleep with one.'

'How do you know that?'

He looked totally flummoxed. 'Well...I just know!'

'You know because you talk to her,' Sarah pointed out harshly. 'Which is more than you ever do with me.'

'For pity's sake, we just talk about business, not personal things. We spend a lot of time together.'

'I am well aware of that,' Sarah said drily.

'Look, this is all getting off the point, which is supposed to be you explaining the content of those photos.'

'I'm just getting to that. I was supposed to meet up with this PI in the hotel bar. But he didn't show up. While we were there, waiting for him, Phil got a call saying that he was tied up watching someone from the balcony of his hotel room upstairs and couldn't come down right at that moment, suggesting we come up instead.'

Scott gave her a sceptical look. 'That doesn't make sense, Sarah. Why couldn't he just tell you whatever he had to tell you over the phone?'

'Phil said he didn't like using mobile phones to relay sensitive information, especially when dealing with celebrities.'

Scott made a scoffing sound. 'So I'm a celebrity now, am I, as well as an adulterer?'

Sarah felt her face flushing. 'I know you're not an adulterer, Scott. The man told me there was absolutely no evidence of your having an affair with Cleo, or any other woman; that he'd watched you for weeks and—'

'Watched me for *weeks*? Good God, what is this? Who hired this guy? Oh, I get it. Leighton hired him, didn't he?'

'Well, yes, he did. Look, I know it all seems a bit odd but it wasn't my idea. Phil's a divorce lawyer and was worried about me after he heard the rumours. He asked his usual investigator to look into it without consulting me.'

'Touting for business, was he? Or was it something more personal than that?'

'I don't know what you're talking about.'

'Haven't you wondered yet who might have sent those photos, Sarah? Blind Freddie can see that if what you say is true, then it had to be a set-up. Luring you to the hotel like that. Getting you to go up to a room. Tell me, was the PI actually in the room when you got up there?'

Sarah frowned. 'No…not at first. He left a note saying he had to step out and follow someone for a few minutes. He didn't arrive till some time later.'

'Making it look like you had enough time to have sex with Leighton before you left.'

Sarah's frown deepened. 'But that would mean that…that…'

'That Leighton was the person who set it all up,' he finished for her.

'But why?'

'Why do you think? He's probably in love with you.'

'Oh, that's ridiculous,' she denied heatedly. Yes, he had invited her out to dinner during the week she'd worked under his mentorship. But only the once. She'd quite enjoyed his company but there'd been no chemistry between them. At least on her part. Then she'd met Scott and Phil had become just a friend. Quite a good friend, actually. Sarah often ran into him in the staff room where she occasionally gave vent to her annoyance at how often Scott went away on business. He was always very sympathetic. Still, it was probably her fault that he thought something had gone wrong with their marriage. But she could see nothing in his behaviour to warrant believing he had romantic feelings towards her. He never flirted, or gave her lustful glances. He never stepped out of line. Ever!

'You're quite wrong,' she stated firmly. 'It has to be someone else. Some woman who's probably in love with Phil and followed us because she was jealous.'

'And what? She just happened to know my phone number?'

'It wouldn't be hard for anyone at work to find out your business number, Scott. It would be in the files.'

'That's a stretch, Sarah. Of course, there is an alternative explanation.'

'What?'

'That you actually *are* having an affair with your work buddy.'

Scott's ongoing distrust hit Sarah like a physical blow. She closed her eyes and shook her head.

'It's a well-known fact that an affair can spice up a bored spouse's libido,' he went on ruthlessly. 'And you were a different woman last Friday night. And then again, today. The virgin I met and married would never have acted like that.'

Her eyes flew open, dismay banished in favour of outrage. 'If you honestly think that, then I feel sorry for you,' she snapped.

'Then how do you explain it?'

'You want the truth?'

'That's exactly what I want.'

'When I was told that you were having an affair with Cleo, I didn't want to believe it, but I still went into a total panic. While I was waiting for the PI's report, I began thinking that maybe you'd grown bored with me in bed—that maybe you'd only married me because I *was* a virgin,' she went on before he could agree with her. 'Anyway, I was so relieved when I found out you weren't having an affair that I actually threw up.'

'God, Sarah.'

'Yes. I know. And yet, when you believed that I was having an affair you came home and proceeded to ravage me endlessly, proving that men and women are totally different creatures.'

Scott grimaced as he thought back to his behaviour last Friday. 'I do regret the way I acted afterwards.'

'Really? I haven't seen much regret. You still believe today that I was having an affair and just look at us! Tearing each other's clothes off. It's madness.' Sarah paused as the weight of her words settled in the silence between them. She needed some space away from Scott, time to gather her thoughts and plan her next steps.

'I'm going to leave, Scott, and I suggest you don't try to stop me.'

He straightened, his broad shoulders squaring as he faced her with narrowed eyes. 'Are you planning on leaving me for good?'

'I don't know yet. We'll have to wait and see.'

'What does that mean, exactly?'

'It means I need some time away from you, Scott. Time to think and to work out what I should do.'

'I don't want you to leave,' he growled. 'Look, I'm sorry for what I did. Sorry I jumped to conclusions. Sorry I acted like a bloody idiot. But we've sorted that out now so there's no need for you to leave. We still love each other, don't we?'

'No,' Sarah said, resisting the temptation to accept his apologies and just stay. 'Scott, we don't even *know* each other. I can see that now. We got married way too quickly. All we have between us is lust. And that's not enough for me. I need to have a husband who truly loves me, and trusts me unconditionally.'

'You expect too much.'

'Perhaps. But I refuse to settle for less.' Her mother had settled for less. And look where that had got her? Dead, at forty-five.

'You didn't trust *me* unconditionally,' he pointed out harshly. 'Underneath, you believed I was having an affair with Cleo.'

A guilty colour crept into her cheeks. 'Then I'm as bad as you. Hardly a good recipe for a happy marriage.' Or good parents, she thought bleakly. Of course, there might not be a baby, but Sarah wasn't hopeful.

Still, she might be lucky...

With a heavy heart, she stood up, putting her shoulders back and facing her husband with as much courage as she could muster. 'I'm going to pack now, Scott, then I'll be leaving. And please...don't try to stop me.'

His top lip curled derisively. 'What point would there be in that? You've clearly already made up your mind to go. To abandon your vows. Did they mean so little to you?'

His barb cut her deeply. She'd meant every one of her vows, but how could she stay with Scott if there was no trust between them? She shot visual daggers at him. 'I'll ignore that,' she bit out. 'But if we keep arguing in this way, Scott, I can't see any hope of a reconciliation.'

'And if you keep working in the same law office as that man, then I feel the same.'

That rocked her. 'You can't possibly expect me to quit my job?'

'You will if you ever want me to take you back.'

His comment stopped Sarah in her tracks and she laughed at the sheer arrogance of her husband. 'Take me *back*? Can you hear what you're saying, Scott? It's *me* who has to decide if I'll take *you* back. And right now, I think the answer to that is a definite no.' Despite her heart breaking into little pieces, she lifted her chin and set defiant eyes upon him. 'I'll be at Cory's,' she said, her voice only wobbling a little. 'I'll let you know what I decide in due course.' Sarah hated that she sounded like a lawyer, but it was the only way she could survive at this moment without breaking down.

Scott sank down onto the nearest chair as Sarah left their apartment, but he didn't try to stop her. His words had been reckless and he could have kicked himself for behaving like such a Neanderthal. Did he not know Sarah at all? Of course she wouldn't respond to such arrogant threats!

Scott felt suddenly powerless and bereft. He had wanted his treacherous wife to leave and now she had. So why did he feel that he had just made the biggest mistake of his life?

CHAPTER FIVE

HALF AN HOUR later Scott headed out to see exactly how much Sarah had taken with her. Just about her whole wardrobe, he noted with a sinking heart, only a few of her long evening gowns left behind. He swore as he ran his hands through his hair. This couldn't be happening to him. They'd been happy. He loved her. And she still loved him, no matter what she'd said. It was all a bloody nightmare!

A tortured groan ripped from Scott's lungs as he faced the fact that Sarah had just actually left him for real. It was one thing to talk about a divorce. Quite another to face the reality of it.

God, but the place seemed so empty without her, he thought despairingly as he made his way back through the bedroom. At the foot of the king-sized bed he stopped, his gaze settling on its crumpled quilt, plus the indentation of where her body had lain. It seemed impossible that just over an hour earlier they'd been on that bed together, making love with a passion that had blown his mind.

Sarah had said that they didn't love each other, that it was just lust, but Scott didn't believe that. He'd experienced plenty of lust in his life and what he felt for

Sarah went way beyond that. He'd loved Sarah from the first moment he'd set eyes on her. Loved her and wanted her like a man possessed.

'And damn it all, I'm going to get her back!' he vowed, and marched down the hallway to what he called his thinking room. Not his study. His gym.

Over the past year whenever Scott was presented with a business problem—and there'd been plenty— he'd come in here, climb up on the exercise bike and pedal away. Not too fast. Just a nice steady rhythm whilst he stared blankly out at the view and set his mind to analysing the problem, usually coming up with a plan of action before too long.

Scott wasn't so optimistic of success this time. He'd finally accepted that his actions last Friday night had been beyond the pale. He hadn't been too nice to Sarah just now as well, letting his temper and his male ego get the better of him. She'd every right to be more than furious with him. He'd really messed things up this time.

Scott suspected that the odds of his securing Sarah's forgiveness any time soon were about the same as the odds of his keeping that nickel refinery open. But he had to try something, or go quietly mad. Changing into his gym gear, he climbed up onto the bike and began to pedal. And pedal. And pedal, his normally pragmatic brain firing up his feet as he struggled with his emotions. Despite knowing that he still loved Sarah, he was also totally frustrated with her.

Why couldn't she see that it was Philip Leighton who'd orchestrated this whole nightmare? It was obvious to him. Why wasn't it obvious to her?

Clearly Leighton was a clever devil, plus an ongoing risk to Scott's goal of getting Sarah back. If she continued to work with him he might somehow poison her mind further. Or come up with some other devious scheme to make trouble for their marriage.

Scott groaned in despair at the realisation that he was powerless to persuade Sarah to quit her job. She wasn't the kind of girl who wilted under fire. She was a courtroom lawyer, after all. But Leighton wasn't the only problem—the startling lack of trust in their marriage would have to be addressed too.

Still, it galled Scott to think of Leighton taking advantage of this moment, hanging around his wife every day at work, worming his way into her affections. If Scott had any chance of saving his marriage, he'd need to speak to Leighton—man to man.

Scowling, he glanced up at the clock—twenty past four. Jumping off the bike, he retrieved his phone from his trouser pocket, brought up the right number and pressed call.

'Goldstein & Evans,' the female receptionist answered. 'How may I help you?'

'Good afternoon. My name is McAllister. Scott McAllister. I was hoping to see Mr Leighton this afternoon.'

'Have you seen Mr Leighton before, Mr McAllister? Are you a client of his?' Clearly, she didn't recognise his name. So much for his being described by Leighton's investigator as a celebrity.

'No. We've never met before.'

'I'm afraid Mr Leighton is busy in a meeting for the rest of the afternoon. I could make an appointment for you to see him later in the week.'

Scott smiled a wry smile. He wasn't about to be

put off by that old 'in a meeting' chestnut. 'That won't do, I'm afraid. I need to see Leighton today. It's urgent. I'm sure he'll see me if you let him know who's calling.'

'Might I ask you the reason you wish to see Mr Leighton?'

'No. It's personal.'

'Personal…'

'Yes. Please tell him that I will be there to see him at five-thirty.' And he hung up.

After a quick shower, Scott put on his new black suit, a crisp white shirt and skinny red tie. Since marrying Sarah his wardrobe had been overhauled and updated, Sarah insisting that he had to look the part if he wanted politicians and wealthy business colleagues to take him seriously. Which he did. He also didn't want to feel in any way inferior to the man he was about to meet. He couldn't help but notice how well dressed the lawyer had been in those photos. Very elegant. Scott knew he could never look elegant. He was much too tall, too broad-shouldered, too big. But he could look impressive. And intimidating. And seriously rich. Which was what he was aiming for.

A final check on his appearance in the vanity mirror left him mostly satisfied. Handsome he would never be but he wasn't ugly by a long shot. His facial features, though on the large side, were symmetrical, his nose was straight and his eyes—which were the same pale grey as his father's—were supposedly sexy. His thick brown hair was annoyingly wayward so he kept it cut very short. He quickly ran a comb through it, glad now that he hadn't shaved, the dark stubble his face was sporting giving his macho looks an added edge. Last but not least he slipped on the gold Rolex wristwatch that he rarely wore but which his father had bought when he'd struck gold two decades earlier. Unfortunately, the mine in question had soon petered out, as had happened with most of his father's finds.

Scott scooped in a deep, gathering breath, picked up his wallet and keys, then set out to do battle with a foe that he vowed not to underestimate. For if he did, things could quickly go belly-up. It was a risk to confront Leighton, but it was a bigger risk to sit back and do nothing. Sarah was upset right now, which could make her vulnerable to a man like Leighton.

Leighton's secretary looked up as he strode into her office, her dark brown eyes showing curiosity as they ran over him. Scott wondered if she knew Sarah; or knew that he was Sarah's husband.

'Mr McAllister, I presume,' she said, smiling as she stood up.

'The one and the same,' he agreed, and smiled back at her.

'Mr Leighton said to take you straight into him the moment you arrived.'

Did he now? Scott thought ruefully as he was shown into his enemy's office.

Leighton was even more handsome in the flesh than in his photos. Handsome and smooth and supremely confident. He came forward to greet Scott with a dazzling smile and hand outstretched. Scott's first reaction was to bypass any pleasantries and just go for the jugular, but he suspected that wouldn't be smart. He had to outmanoeuvre this slime bag, not fall into any of his traps. And there would be traps,

Scott was sure of it. So he took the offered hand and resisted the temptation to crush all his elegant fingers to pulp.

'So pleased to finally meet you, Scott,' Leighton said, doing the old politician's trick of covering their handshake with his other hand, aping a false warmth. 'Sarah has told me so much about you.'

'Really? She hasn't mentioned you,' Scott said, his iron control slipping a little as he pulled his hand away.

A mistake, he quickly realised, Leighton's brows lifting as though he was puzzled by his visitor's attitude.

'I see,' he said slowly, giving a good impression of working out why Scott might want an urgent appointment with a divorce lawyer. 'Would I be right in assuming you're seeking my help in a professional capacity?'

You wish, Scott almost snapped, but held his tongue just in time.

'Actually no,' Scott was pleased to announce. 'That's not why I'm here at all.' And he handed him the phone with the first of the many photos already on the screen. 'I've come to ask if you have any explanations for these photos that were sent to me last Friday afternoon.'

Leighton frowned as he scanned through the photos before glancing up at Scott, his expression seemingly shocked. 'Has Sarah seen these?' was his first question.

'Of course.'

'What did she say?'

Scott recounted Sarah's explanation, letting Leighton think he'd shown her the photos last Friday, not the next morning.

'And you believed her?' he said, sounding surprised.

'Of course,' Scott retorted, ignoring the stab of guilt which accompanied the lie. 'Sarah would never lie to me.'

'Of course not,' the oily bastard said with a smirk. 'If that's what Sarah said happened, then that's exactly what happened.'

Scott adopted his best poker face. '*You* sent me those photos,' he said, his quietly controlled voice a credit to him, considering how furious he was inside. But Scott knew it was never a good idea to let an enemy see weakness. And losing one's temper made a man look weak.

Leighton was clearly taken aback at the unexpectedness of Scott's accusation. 'Why would I do something like that?'

'The why is obvious,' he returned smoothly. 'You want my wife for yourself and you're prepared to do anything to have her, even set her up so that it looks like she was having an affair with you.'

The man actually smiled. 'I'd be careful what you say in the presence of a lawyer, if I were you. That could constitute slander.'

Oh, yes, he was a clever bastard. But Scott was ready for him. 'Don't threaten me, Leighton,' he countered coolly. 'Give me forty-eight hours and I'll know all there is to know about you. All your dirty little secrets.'

Suddenly, Leighton didn't look quite so confident, or so handsome. His cheeks puffed out, his close-

set eyes darkening as he blinked incessantly. 'I...
I've done nothing to be ashamed of,' he blustered before suddenly pulling himself together, clearing his
throat and straightening his tie before speaking again.
'You're nothing but a rough-neck bully, McAllister.
Sarah would be better off without you. You think
I haven't worked out what happened when you got
those photos and that telling little text? You didn't
believe Sarah at all. You came storming home and
did something awful to her. That's probably why she
didn't come to work today. Because she's sporting a
black eye. Or worse.'

'I would never hit Sarah,' Scott said with cold fury,
though he was close to hitting *him*. Still, he had been
close to the mark. He *hadn't* believed in Sarah and
Scott already knew that he would have to work very
hard to get her to forgive him. If she ever did, that
was. Meanwhile, this manipulative creep wasn't about
to go away. But he'd tripped himself up just now.

'How did you know about the text that came with
the photos?' Scott asked. 'I deleted it before I came
here.'

Leighton just smiled. 'What text? I know nothing of any text. Now I think this meeting is over,' he
stated with an arrogance that needled Scott no end.
'Unless, of course, you have something else to say.'

Scott smiled, but somehow he restrained himself.
'Stay away from my wife.'

Leighton smirked again. 'That's up to Sarah, don't
you think? Or do you plan on dictating who she can
have as friends in future? That's the usual tactic for
bully-boy husbands.'

'You're a dead man.' The unwise words fell out of

Scott's mouth before he could stop them. Furious at his stupidity, Scott whirled and marched over to the door, flinging it open then striding quickly past the wide-eyed brunette. He didn't have the satisfaction of seeing the fear that filled Leighton's eyes, or the way the coward slumped down in a nearby chair, his legs having gone to jelly.

CHAPTER SIX

'So let me get this straight,' Cory said as he set out the Chinese food on the breakfast bar in the upstairs kitchen. 'Scott was there when you came out of the shower, after which you had fantastic make-up sex, but didn't make up at all, despite you telling him what really happened at the hotel last Friday and his eventually believing you. Did I get that right?'

'It was never make-up sex,' Sarah refuted heatedly. 'It was just sex.'

'Right,' Cory said slowly, then shook his head at her. 'Not like you, sweetie.'

'No,' she choked out, on the verge of tears again. 'I don't know what's got into me. Ever since last Friday night all I can think about is having sex with that bastard.'

Cory's eyebrows arched. 'Really? Wow. Okay, so what's your problem, then? Why are you here instead of at home in bed with Brutus?'

Sarah grimaced. 'You don't understand, Cory. I married Scott because I was in love with him and I thought he was in love with me. Now I'm not sure he ever loved me.'

'Rubbish. He's always been crazy about you.'

'That's not the same as love. If he truly loved me, and believed I truly loved him, then he would have trusted me. And respected me more. I didn't see any evidence of either last Friday.'

'Oh, come now, Sarah, be reasonable. The man was mad with jealousy at the time. You're a lawyer. You know about temporary insanity. Cut the poor guy some slack.'

'So now he's a poor guy instead of Brutus, is he? You men sure do stick together.'

Cory gave her a droll look. 'I'm just trying to make you see his side of the story. Look, let's start eating this food before it gets cold. What do you think of the wine?'

Sarah automatically lifted her glass to her lips before she remembered that she might be pregnant. Wincing, she put the glass back down again.

'What is it?' Cory asked immediately. 'Is it off?' He picked up his glass and took a sip. 'Nope. Tastes great.'

Sarah suppressed a groan. She hadn't wanted to tell Cory about her pregnancy scare but he was too intelligent to fool for long. 'I...I can't have any alcohol,' she told him reluctantly. 'Not till I find out if I'm expecting a baby or not.'

That floored him. Sarah knew exactly how he felt.

'But you're on the pill,' he said, clearly perplexed.

'I've forgotten to take it lately,' she confessed, still shaken by this realisation. She sighed a heavy sigh. 'Like I said, I'm not myself. My brains have been well and truly scrambled.'

Cory pulled a face. 'Am I right in presuming you didn't tell Scott you'd forgotten to take the pill?'

'Are you mad?' Sarah said, then shuddered. 'Of course I didn't tell him. No way.'

'But why, Sarah? The possibility of your having a baby together might help solve all your problems.'

A weary sigh puffed from Sarah's lungs. 'Spoken like a man again. Having a baby doesn't solve a relationship problem, Cory. If anything it complicates things. Women don't have to marry these days just because they're pregnant. They don't have to stay married, either.'

Cory looked taken aback. 'You're thinking of actually divorcing Scott?'

Just the thought of divorcing Scott made Sarah feel nauseous. 'I didn't say that,' she hedged. 'But I need to step back from my marriage for a while and do some clear thinking.' She sure as hell couldn't think clearly when she was around Scott.

'Perhaps that's not such a bad idea,' Cory said thoughtfully. 'Like they say, distance makes the heart grow fonder. Now eat up. You could be eating for two, remember?'

She ate the food in thoughtful silence, not really tasting it, her mind elsewhere.

A baby, she started thinking. A real live baby. She had always wanted to start a family with Scott, but not like this. So why hadn't she dashed out and bought a morning-after pill today? Why had she just come home here and cried her eyes out, like some helpless idiot?

Because it was too late to do anything now. She couldn't remember the last time she had taken a pill, so reckless she'd been! What a mess she had made of her life.

'You're quite welcome to stay here as long as you like,' Cory offered after they'd finished eating and they were clearing up together. 'There's been a delay in starting the renovations so things will be staying the same for a good while yet.'

'Thank you, darling,' she said, and came round to give him a hug. 'You are such a good friend.'

'True,' he said with a smile.

The front doorbell ringing made his smile fade. 'If that's Felix come to beg my forgiveness then he hasn't a hope in hell.'

Sarah laughed. 'You know you always forgive him in the end.'

'That's because I'm a Libra,' he said soulfully as he headed for the stairs. 'Wish I was a Scorpio, like you. Then I would invite him in for a drink, tip some hemlock into his glass from my poison ring and send him on his way.'

Scott heard Sarah's laughter from where he was standing outside Cory's front door. Not totally broken-hearted by their separation then, he thought rather bitterly. Unlike himself. Maybe he'd been right when he wondered if she'd kept her virginity to ensnare herself a rich husband. Maybe she now planned to take him to the cleaners in the divorce court.

And maybe you should stop thinking like some suspicious jealous fool and set about doing what you came here for. Getting the woman you love back!

'Scott!' Cory exclaimed on opening the door. 'It isn't Felix,' he called up the stairs. 'It's Scott.'

No more laughter now. Just silence.

'Come in,' Cory said. 'Sarah and I have just finished eating. No food left I'm afraid but I can offer you some wine…'

'I just came to talk to Sarah,' Scott said stiffly, not sure what to make of the drily amused tone in Cory's voice.

'She's upstairs in the kitchen. I dare say you'll want to be alone. I'll go down the local for a while,' he added, grabbing a jacket from the coat rack on the wall and disappearing out of the front door.

Scott was making his way up the steep steps when Sarah appeared at the top of the staircase. Her arms were crossed and her expression was not happy.

'I thought I told you not to contact me,' she said sharply. 'I said I would contact you when I was ready.'

Anger did become her, he thought, noting her wildly glittering eyes and high colour. She'd looked like that this afternoon when he'd been inside her. There was something about Sarah in a temper that stirred the caveman in him. The temptation to ignore her hostile body language and just sweep her into his arms was acute. He liked the thought of her fighting him, of her lashing out at first. He would welcome her blows. Absorb them. Be aroused by them. Scott felt confident that she would surrender to him in the end. But at what cost afterwards? He'd come to reason with her, not ravage her.

Scott shoved his hands into his trouser pockets, ignoring his erection and adopting a composed demeanour. 'I assumed you might like to know what happened when I dropped in on Leighton just now,' he said in a creditably calm voice.

Sarah sucked in sharply, her arms falling away to

her sides. 'You *didn't*!' she exclaimed, not sure if she was annoyed or thrilled.

'What did you expect, Sarah? That I would not confront the man who's meddling in our marriage?'

'What…what did Phil say?'

The muscles under Scott's granite-like jaw tightened considerably. 'Look, I have no intention of having this conversation standing on a staircase. Either you come down or I'll come up.'

'I'll come down,' Sarah said, then wished she hadn't. Far better that she have Scott sitting safely on the other side of the breakfast bar than next to her on Cory's large squashy lounge. But she could hardly change her mind now. Scott had already whirled and was stomping down the wooden steps.

Sarah followed him into Cory's far too cosy living room, switching on the overhead lights as she did so, despite there being two corner lamps on already. The last thing she needed right now was to be seduced by a romantic ambience. Bad enough that just the sight of Scott in that brilliant black suit had her practically salivating with desire for him. Weird. She'd chosen that particular suit for him because she'd wanted him to look more sophisticated during his business meetings. More…impressive. Looking sexy had not been on her agenda. But he looked more than sexy in it tonight. He looked…dangerous.

When Scott plonked himself down in the middle of the maroon velvet sofa, Sarah chose an adjacent armchair, perching on the end of it without a shred of her usual social grace. Clasping her hands nervously on her jeans-clad thighs, she swallowed, then leant even further forward.

'So what did he say?' she asked, driven by equal measures of anxiety and curiosity.

'He backed up your story,' Scott replied, his eyes not leaving hers.

A rush of relieved air escaped from Sarah's tightly held chest.

'I could have told you he would. Because it's the truth. Did you, um, show him the photos?'

'I did.'

'I'll bet he was shocked.'

'Not nearly shocked enough,' Scott said drily. 'On top of that, he mentioned the text that came with the photos. Yet I'd already deleted that.'

'I…I don't understand…'

Scott's face filled with exasperation. 'What's not to understand, Sarah? It's plain as the nose on your face. Leighton set you up, then organised for those photos to be taken. *He* sent them, along with the text.'

'I still find that hard to believe.' And she did.

'Believe it, because it's true.'

'But *why*?'

'Leighton is an ambitious bastard. He has his eyes on a career in politics and to be successful you need the right kind of wife. And you fit the bill, darling, in every way. You have the looks, the poise and the smarts. You're a girl in a million.'

Sarah ignored the flattery in his words and concentrated on the heart of the matter. 'But to do what you say he's done is just so evil!'

'It worked, though. You left me.'

'It wouldn't have worked if you'd trusted me.'

Scott's sigh was heavy. 'I know, but surely you can

appreciate how bad things looked. Any man would have been worried.'

'Worried. Yes. But that's no excuse for what you did last Friday night. You should have shown me those photos as soon as you got home.'

Scott smothered a groan. 'Do we have to go through this all again? Look, I know I was wrong and I'm sorry. I made a mistake. All you have to do is come home and we can work through this. We still love each other, Sarah. You know we do. Look what happened today.'

How could she forget? She only had to look at him to remember every mind-blowing moment. She could still feel the effects of that orgasm, deep in her body. Sarah struggled with the various emotions bombarding her; not the least was the temptation to surrender all her pride and common sense, and just say yes. *Yes, I'll come home. Yes, we'll go on as if none of this has ever happened.*

But she couldn't. Because that was what her mother had done. Continuously forgiven the unforgivable and taken her husband back. Sarah now suspected she had a clue as to why she'd done that—the pull of sexual desire and physical satisfaction. But she refused to do that with Scott, no matter how exciting a lover he'd become. A marriage could not be founded on lust alone. It needed love to survive.

'I can't do that, Scott,' she said. 'I'm not ready to come back just yet.'

'When will you be ready, then?' he asked softly.

'I'm not sure I'll ever be ready.'

Sarah was taken aback by the look of horror on his face.

'You don't mean that,' he said, clearly shaken. 'You have to give me a second chance.'

Sarah steeled herself to stay strong. 'I don't *have* to do any such thing, Scott. Like I said, I need time away from you just now.'

Scott sighed and ran his hands through his hair. 'Fair enough. How long do you need?'

How long? Maybe after she found out if she was pregnant or not, she could come to a decision. If there was to be a baby, it would be wrong not to make an effort to fix things between them. Maybe the lust that seemed to be all she felt for Scott at this moment could turn back to love...

'Two weeks,' she said. She would know for sure in two weeks.

Scott looked horrified. 'Two weeks? That's one hell of a long time.'

'Not really.'

'And will you be going back to work during that time?'

'Of course. I'll be going back tomorrow.' And going to see Phil too. She suspected Scott was telling the truth and that Phil was behind those photos, but she wanted to speak to him first to get his side of the story.

'How can you work with someone who set you up like that?'

'I don't work with Phil, Scott,' she pointed out archly. 'He just works at the same firm. I don't have to see him if I don't want to.'

'But you do want to, don't you? You'll run off and see him first thing in the morning.'

Sarah stiffened, her back straightening as her chin

lifted. 'I think I have the same right to confront him as you. To give him the opportunity to give me his version of events.'

'God, I have to get out of here before I say or do something I'll seriously regret,' Scott said, jumping to his feet. 'Two weeks you said? Okay, I'll give you two weeks. But after that I'm done with this marriage.'

Scott's statement shocked her to the core. She'd imagined he would always be there for her if she wanted him.

Sarah stood up to face her very frustrated-looking husband. 'Scott, I...I...' She didn't have a clue what to say. She just hated him looking at her the way he was presently looking at her.

'You don't have to say anything, Sarah. I get the picture. I'm to be made to suffer for what I've done. I can understand you wanting to leave me—I've behaved badly, but I've apologised for that. What I don't understand is why you would continue to associate with the bastard who caused all this trouble in the first place. You want my trust, but won't do me the courtesy of having nothing to do with Leighton. I'm beginning to suspect that you never loved me at all— perhaps this is what you always wanted. A divorce after a suitable time span and a gravy-train alimony which will set you up for life.'

'That's not true!' she denied, horrified. Little did he know it but she didn't need his money. She had quite a bit of her own, inherited after her mother died. How else could she have travelled the world for two years after her mother's funeral?

Of course, he didn't know that. She hadn't told

him. It had been her own secret nest egg, her safety net in case her marriage hadn't worked out.

And it hadn't, had it?

'I don't want any of your damned money,' she threw at him.

'What do you want, then?'

'A husband who loves and trusts me! Look, Scott, we are going around in circles arguing like this. I just think we need some time apart. I'll call you after two weeks and we'll talk.'

He swore, then shook his head at her. His laugh smacked of frustration. 'I don't need any time apart. I want you home, in my bed and in my arms.'

Sarah hated the way her body reacted to his impassioned words. It wanted the same thing. But she knew it wasn't the right thing to do. Scott would think she was weak. Which was what she'd been so far where he was concerned. In the past, she'd given in to whatever he wanted to do. She hadn't made a fuss when he'd kept going away on business. She hadn't insisted he take her with him sometimes, like that last time when he'd only been going to a hotel on the Gold Coast. She'd bitterly resented his taking Cleo. Sarah knew she should have said something instead of pretending she didn't mind.

But she refused to play the compliant, accommodating little wife any longer. It was time to make her stand.

'I'm sorry, Scott,' she said staunchly, 'but that won't be happening. I believe I have the right to ask for this small space of time. Please respect my wishes. I'll be in contact after the two weeks are up.'

He stared at her as if he couldn't believe this was

happening to him. But his shocked expression soon changed to a sullen anger and he stormed out of the house, slamming the front door as he did so.

A stunned Sarah staggered over to the sofa and slumped down in the middle of it, all the breath leaving her lungs. She shuddered to think what he'd say if she ever had to tell him she was pregnant, but she'd kept the possibility a secret from him.

Oh, God. A baby was a complication she didn't need right now. She needed to sort her marriage out without feeling pressured to make unwise decisions. She needed Scott to stay well away from her.

The front door opening and closing had Sarah's back stiffening against the sofa. But it wasn't Scott. It was Cory.

'I just saw Scott roaring up the road like some kind of maniac,' her friend said as he sat down next to her. 'I gather, by the look on your face, you didn't sort anything out.'

'Oh, Cory,' Sarah cried unhappily, then burst into tears.

CHAPTER SEVEN

A SET OF red lights forced Scott to abandon his suicidal speed. He still slammed his hands against the steering wheel, angry more with himself than Sarah. He'd lost his temper. That was the long and the short of it. Though, damn it all, she *was* being very difficult. How did she think he felt about having her work in the same place as that slime ball?

Still, he hadn't handled that at all well, had he? Not that negotiation was ever his strong point. He hated having to manipulate people, or promise to deliver things that down deep he knew he couldn't deliver. Which was what being a businessman was all about. He much preferred the simple life of a miner. Mining was cut and dried. You either had a mine worth mining or you didn't.

Scott imagined marriage was pretty much like a mine. You either had one worth keeping, or you didn't. Till this last hiccup, Sarah had been a wonderful wife. He couldn't have asked for better. His accusation that she'd married him for his money did not ring true. A materialistic woman wouldn't have refused his offer of a free credit card and a generous monthly allowance, the way Sarah had. She'd have taken everything he was offering, instead of adopting an independent stance, informing him that she earned a good salary and preferred to pay for her own clothes and things.

The lights turned green and Scott drove on more slowly, his mind turning over as he tried to work out what Sarah wanted from him other than more abject apologies. If he thought flowers and diamonds would work, he'd try them, but he suspected such gestures would cement him as being one of those husbands who thought he could buy his wife's forgiveness and affection. Which left what? Communication, he supposed. Women did like to talk. But how could he talk to her when she'd forbidden him to contact her?

Two weeks. Two long bloody awful weeks. He hadn't been two weeks without Sarah since their wedding night. He hadn't been a *week*. Even when away on business, he would ring her every night and tell her how much he loved her and missed her. Scott ached to call her right now but he knew without even trying her number that she would not answer.

Two weeks. He was going to go stark raving mad!

Sarah cried on and off all night, the next morning seeing her so drained and puffy-eyed that she rang in sick again. Of course, this time she would have to get a doctor's certificate, the firm she worked for being very strict about such things. In a way she was glad that she wouldn't be going into work. She didn't want to face Phil just yet. To discover he was behind the problems in her marriage and to tell him exactly what she thought of him. On top of that, she could ask the doctor when she could reasonably take a pregnancy test.

Cory gave her the number of his local surgery but she wasn't able to get an appointment till late that afternoon. By the time Sarah was ushered in to see the doctor shortly after five, she was feeling both anxious and stressed. Going to the doctor always made her feel that way. But the elderly lady doctor was very nice, taking her blood pressure then listening to Sarah carefully as she explained that her marriage was going through a difficult time, that she was now temporarily separated from her husband but was worried that she might have fallen pregnant.

The doctor frowned at her. 'I hope you don't take this the wrong way, Mrs McAllister, but is the reason for your separation anything to do with domestic or sexual abuse?'

'Good God, no!' Sarah blurted out.

'Sorry. But I had to ask. Over the years I have seen lots of women in my surgery who are victims of such things, and I have to check this isn't the case with you.'

'No—no. The sex between us is fine. I just… We just… Well, it's hard to explain.'

'I understand. Would you like to see a marriage guidance counsellor, perhaps?'

Sarah knew instinctively that Scott wouldn't agree to that.

'Not just yet,' she hedged. 'Not until I find out if I'm pregnant or not. When do you think I will know for certain?'

'Probably not for another week at least. It takes a while for the egg to be implanted in the lining of the womb, which then releases the hormone that the test is looking for. There is a blood test you could take but I see no reason for that. Best to just wait till your next period is due then use one of the home testing kits you can buy over the counter. They're quite reliable. There's no need to come back to see me. I understand you don't actually live in this area. Meanwhile...' She picked up a pad and jotted something down on it before giving it to Sarah. 'I would suggest you take one of these vitamin tablets daily. They have folic acid in them. Also keep off the alcohol. Do you smoke?'

'No.'

'Good. Now, do you need a doctor's certificate for today?'

'Yes, I do. I didn't sleep much last night and I simply couldn't go to work this morning.'

'You do look tired. And I can see you're quite stressed. Your blood pressure is up too. I think, under the circumstances, that you should take the rest of the week off. I won't give you any sleeping tablets but I want you to rest. Watch TV. Read a book or two.'

Sarah doubted she could read at the moment but she liked the idea of resting and watching TV.

'Thank you so much,' she said when the nice doctor wrote out the certificate.

'My pleasure,' the woman said, and smiled at her. 'Look after yourself, dear. And come back, if you ever want to.'

'Ah, you saw Dr Jenkins, did you?' Cory said when Sarah relayed her visit in detail that evening. 'She's a love. Getting a bit long in the tooth but still very with it.'

'I liked her a lot. Now what are we going to eat tonight?'

'Search me. Pizza do? I don't feel like cooking.'

'Neither do I. But I'll cook tomorrow night.'

A phone started to ring, Sarah recognising the tone immediately. She retrieved her phone from her bag and saw that it was Scott. Her breathing quickened, just seeing his name. Her heart wanted to answer him, but her head stepped in and said no. He had to learn to respect her wishes. But it was with some regret—and a smattering of guilt—that she switched off the phone.

'Scott, I presume?' Cory asked.

'Yes.'

'So when are you going to tell him about the baby?'

'When there *is* a baby, Cory. Not before.'

'I didn't realise you could be this tough.'

'Neither did I,' she said with some surprise.

'Poor Scott.'

'There's nothing poor about Scott,' she said ruefully.

'True. Still, I wouldn't wait too long to tell him, if it turns out you *are* pregnant. Scott's not a man who likes to be kept in the dark.'

Sarah blinked as Cory's words sank in and she imagined telling Scott the news about a baby. For all his anger and arrogance, Scott would be a wonderful father. But would he welcome the news of a child conceived during the darkest moments of their marriage, or would it spell the end for good? For a moment, Sarah felt a faint chill run down her spine. Only time would tell.

CHAPTER EIGHT

By Friday that week Scott was tearing his hair out. And so was Cleo.

'You can't go on like this,' she told him as she walked into his office and deposited another mega-sized coffee on his desk. 'All you do is drink coffee when you should be seeing about your cash-flow problems. If you don't do something about it soon, your whole business might go down the tubes.'

'I don't give a hoot about the business,' he growled, and meant it. Which shocked him. But not as much as the apparent disintegration of his marriage. 'All I care about is Sarah.'

'Then ring her, for pity's sake!'

'I've tried. She's switched her phone off.'

'Then go and see her. It's not as though you don't know where she is.'

'If I thought a personal visit would work, I would. But you didn't see her the other night. She'd just slam the door in my face.'

'What on earth did you do to make her so mad at you?' Cleo asked.

Scott sighed. 'Aside from my myriad mistakes where the photos were concerned, I suspect it was my demanding she quit her job which put the tin hat on everything.'

'Oh, dear,' Cleo said, and shook her head. 'Never a good idea to make your wife's decisions for her, especially about her career. Sarah is an intelligent girl, Scott, who can make her own decisions. It sounds like you just come over as a controlling husband. Trust me when I tell you that's not the way to a girl's heart.'

Scott was taken aback by the note of irony in Cleo's voice. 'Sounds like you have some experience with controlling husbands.'

An unhappy flicker flashed through her eyes. A memory of something not at all pleasant. 'My father-in-law was not a nice man to live with,' she said. 'He was very possessive. Very controlling. He made life… difficult…for his family.'

Scott frowned. 'But I thought he died before you even met Martin.'

'He did. But Doreen has told me a lot about him.'

'I see.' Scott knew that Cleo's mother-in-law lived with her nowadays, having moved in after her son's death from cancer three years earlier. From what he gathered they were very fond of one another. Very close.

Thinking of fondness and closeness catapulted an image of Sarah back into his mind. Scott suppressed a groan at the thought that he wouldn't be able to even *talk* to her for another ten days. How on earth would he cope? Already he was drinking too much every evening. And eating loads of junk food. He didn't even feel like exercising any more. As for work…he hadn't been lying when he told Cleo he wasn't interested in work. He wasn't.

The trouble was it wasn't just him depending on McAllister Mines. Thousands of employees were relying on his keeping his company solvent, people he liked and valued. To continue to neglect the business was close to criminal. Some of his other varied investments would probably survive—he'd put quite a bit into real estate over the years—but a couple of the mines, plus the nickel refinery, needed money now, and plenty of it.

'I suppose I can't ignore the business for ever,' Scott said with a sigh. Much as he would like to at the moment. 'So! How are you going with finding me another silent partner? One with more money than sense.'

Cleo's face lit up as it did when she became involved in a research project. 'The best one I've been able to find is Byron Maddox, only son and heir to the Maddox Media Empire. During his twenties, he worked for his father as an executive but they parted company—business-wise—a few years back. Now he has his own company, called the BM Group. It's not on the stock exchange but is reputably doing very well. *Business Review Weekly* listed him as number eleven on Australia's rich list in June last year. Technically he's not a billionaire yet but close to.'

Scott nodded. He'd actually met Byron Maddox at the races one day last year and had liked him. The man definitely had charisma, and loads of smarts. Maybe too many. Still, as the saying went, beggars couldn't be choosers.

'Okay,' he agreed. 'Set up a meeting with him ASAP.'

'Already onto it, boss. Unfortunately, the man himself is in America at the moment. Family business according to his PA. Anyway, he'll be back in Sydney at his head office early next week. She's going to get back to me with a suitable date and time for you two to meet.'

'Excellent. Whatever would I do without you, Cleo?'

'You'd be broke. And I'd be unemployed.'

'Not for long,' he muttered, picked up his coffee and took a deep swallow. He didn't see Cleo's exasperated eyes, or the determined set of her mouth. Neither could he read her mind. Which was just as well.

Sarah had just eaten an omelette—Cory was away in Melbourne on a weekend architectural conference—and was packing up the dishwasher when the doorbell rang.

The sound sent electric currents charging through her veins. It was Scott. She just knew it was Scott.

What to do? Ignore it? Pretend no one was home?

A bit difficult with the TV on downstairs as well as most of the lights.

Whilst she stood there, waffling, the doorbell rang again. This time she turned and made it to the top of the stairs before stopping, hotly aware of her galloping heart and churning stomach.

A voice suddenly shouted through the door. 'It's just me, Sarah. Cleo. Please let me in.'

'Cleo…' A whoosh of air puffed from Sarah's lungs as she hurried down the steps and along to the front door. She didn't even stop to think what her husband's PA could possibly be doing here, she was so glad it wasn't the man himself.

Sweeping the door open, she almost gave the woman a hug. But one look at Cleo's somewhat grim face made her step back in alarm.

'What is it?' she asked straight away. 'Is it Scott? Has he been hurt?'

The look Cleo gave her was not one Sarah was used to seeing on Scott's PA. Whilst Cleo in general was not an overly smiley person, neither was she a grump. Right at that moment, however, she looked very grumpy indeed, her big brown eyes narrowed, her nicely shaped lips pursed with displeasure.

'If you mean has he been hurt in some sort of accident,' Cleo said sharply, 'then no, he hasn't. But he's hurting all right. Hurting so much that he can hardly put two sensible thoughts together. I couldn't stand the prospect of another week of watching the poor man suffer so I decided to come here tonight and try to talk some sense into you.'

The censorious tone of Cleo's words pricked at Sarah's pride, plus her temper. Who did Cleo think she was, coming here like this and criticising her actions? The jealousy that had been simmering away in Sarah for some weeks infuriated her further. But before she could fashion a suitably cutting reply, Cleo's face softened, her next words full of self-reproach.

'I'm sorry. That was uncalled for. I know you love Scott. And I know he must have done or said something awful to make you leave him. But he hasn't been himself since he got those photos. I just…well…I just had to try to do something to make things right between you two. He doesn't have anyone else to speak up for him, you know. No parents or close friends. All he has is you.'

'And you,' Sarah said, her own attitude softening. 'Not really. I'm just his PA.'

Sarah sighed. 'I think you're way more than that, Cleo. He often speaks of you. He admires you enormously.' Which was true. It sometimes irked Sarah how much he complimented Cleo.

'Scott's a good man,' Cleo said. 'And a great boss. He actually cares about the people who work for him, which is a rare commodity in this day and age. Not this last week, though. He's lost all interest in the business.'

This final piece of news amazed Sarah. She could never have imagined anything interfering with Scott's work ethic. But it was some comfort to hear that the problems they were having had affected him to such an extent. Maybe he did love her after all. Love, however, wore many faces, Sarah knew from experience. The kind of love she wanted from Scott had to include trust, and respect, not just physical attraction.

'I'm sorry to hear that,' Sarah said. 'But he's brought all this on himself. Look, I don't know how much you know about what happened. Though clearly, Scott confides in you,' she added a little waspishly. 'Why else would you be here? I mean, you obviously knew where to come to find me.'

'Scott does not *confide* in me,' Cleo denied somewhat sternly. 'But I can't help gleaning things in my position. Look, do you think I could come in? Not only is it chilly out here, but there's something I wish to say to you. In private,' she said quietly, glancing around at the people who were walking by on the pavement, one of whom went into the house next door, throwing them a curious glance as he did so.

Sarah didn't want to be lectured by her husband's PA, but neither did she want to be rude to her. She liked Cleo, on the whole. But she did envy her position in Scott's life, a position that contained more true intimacy than she had. He spent more time with his PA than his wife; took her away on business trips with him; asked her opinion on things. No doubt she'd seen those appalling photos and jumped to the same horrid conclusions. It was obvious that her sympathies were all with Scott.

With some reluctance Sarah led her into the downstairs lounge room, switching off the TV whilst Cleo seated herself on the sofa. It was warmer inside the double-brick building, but Sarah still switched on the electric heater that sat in the old fireplace and looked a bit like a real fire, with faux black coals surrounded by fake flames.

'Would you like some coffee?' Sarah asked with arms crossed. 'Or a glass of wine perhaps?' There was plenty in the fridge, Sarah no longer imbibing. This thought reminded her of the pregnancy testing kit that she'd bought today, despite knowing it was still too soon to get a reliable result, though the salesgirl in the chemist shop told her that this new test could detect a pregnancy earlier than the older ones.

How long, Sarah wondered, before temptation would get the better of her and she'd take the test?

'No, I don't want anything to drink,' Cleo replied brusquely. 'I won't be staying long. I see that you're not happy with my coming here. But I simply *had* to come.'

The intensity in her voice—and in her eyes—had Sarah uncrossing her arms and sinking down on the sofa next to her. Without thinking, she reached out to touch the distressed woman on the hand.

'I'm sorry,' Sarah said softly. 'I'm not normally this rude. What do you want to say to me about Scott? I promise that I'll listen.'

'It's not just about Scott. It's about marriage.'

Sarah blinked. 'What about marriage?'

Cleo shook her head, her dark eyes clouding over. 'It's hard, Sarah. Being married. Very hard, especially when your husband doesn't treat you right...' Her voice drifted off, as did her gaze.

Sarah frowned, wondering if she was talking about her own marriage. Yet according to Scott, Cleo had been a devoted wife. She'd certainly not become a merry widow, that was for sure. But was that because her marriage had been supremely happy, or simply horrid?

Cleo appeared to give herself a mental shake, as though forcing herself out of her bleak thoughts and back to the problem at hand.

'Be thankful,' she said firmly, 'that you have a husband who is alive and well and who loves you more than anything else in the world. He might not be perfect but then are you? Scott knows he jumped to a wrong conclusion about those photos and is truly sorry. So please, give him a second chance, Sarah. He deserves it. Talk to him, at least.'

Sarah grimaced. 'I really don't know what to say to him right now.'

'Well, nothing is being achieved with what you're doing. By the time you're ready to talk to Scott he might not be ready to talk to you. Look, communication is the answer to a good relationship. You must talk to Scott, tell him all your hopes and fears. Make him tell you his. Let down all your defences—and your pride—and tell each other everything. Make him see what you want in life, and in a husband. I'm sure he's up to the challenge, Sarah, because he does truly love you. And I know you truly love him.'

'How do you know that?' Sarah threw at her, both inspired and anguished by her advice. For how could she tell Scott *everything*? Some things were too private, too…shameful, in a way.

Cleo's smile was soft. 'One only has to see you two together to know. It's in the way you look at each other. It's all in your eyes.'

Sarah wasn't so sure about that. She'd learnt last weekend that what she'd seen in Scott's eyes was good old lust, not love. The same with herself. Maybe that was all it had ever been. That, combined with companionship, plus the added bonus of not having to worry about money. Lots of marriages faltered on the matter of money. She wondered what Cleo's husband had done before he got cancer. Whether money had been a problem for them. Not that she would ever ask. But she suspected their marriage might not have been the utopia Scott had always implied it had been.

'Promise me that you will at least call him,' Cleo urged. 'Tonight. Don't wait. You don't have to rush back to him, if that's not what you want. But at least talk to him, Sarah. Please.'

Sarah still didn't really want to talk to Scott. Not yet. But after what Cleo had told her about Scott's distraught state of mind, to not do so would brand her a coward, and very cruel. Hopefully, she was neither.

But she would not be going back to him. Not yet. Not till she knew if there was to be a baby.

And maybe not even then...

'All right,' she said, though her reluctance was obvious.

'Promise me,' Cleo repeated firmly.

'I promise.'

'Tonight?'

'Yes. Tonight.'

Cleo heaved a huge sigh of relief as she stood up. 'Thank you,' she said.

Sarah levered herself up also. 'Are you sure I can't get you anything?'

'No. I've done what I came for. I'll be going now. Oh, but before I go, could you promise me something else?'

'What?' Sarah asked with a hint of impatience.

'Don't tell Scott I came to see you. He wouldn't be at all happy with me.'

'All right, then,' Sarah said, privately agreeing with Cleo's request. It made sense. Scott would not like to think that his PA was meddling in his private life. 'I won't mention your visit.'

When Cleo smiled, Sarah saw how very attractive the woman could be with the right clothes, plus the right hairstyle and make-up. Quite stunning really. Not that she wanted her to be stunning, Sarah conceded as she saw Cleo out. Not with the amount of time she spent with Scott. Far better that she looked her usual bland and rather boring self.

By the time Sarah closed the front door behind Cleo she was frowning, troubled by the realisation that she still felt jealous of the woman, despite it being obvious that there was nothing for her to be jealous about. Her mother had been a very jealous woman, she recalled. Obsessively so. Sarah wondered if the tendency to jealousy was an inherited factor. She didn't want to be jealous. She hated how it twisted a person's mind and made them miserable.

Of course, her mother had had every reason to be jealous, with her husband being a philanderer of the worst kind. Her mother used to excuse her frequent temper tantrums by saying it was because she loved Sarah's father so much. Sarah's frown deepened as she trudged slowly up the steep stairs. Was obsessive jealousy linked with obsessive love? She didn't like that concept. Didn't like it at all.

Sarah straightened her shoulders and lifted her chin, steadfastly ignoring the deep well of insecurity that had plagued her ever since her parents' divorce, not to mention her mother's suicide. The doctor had called her mother's overdose an accident, a combination of prescription pills and alcohol. But Sarah knew differently. Her mother had killed herself, all because her chronically unfaithful husband hadn't loved her. Had *never* loved her. According to her mother he'd only married her because she fell pregnant. Not with Sarah herself, with her older brother, Victor. Then, when her husband had started to seriously stray, her mother had tried to keep him by having another baby. *Her.*

Babies didn't strengthen a bad marriage, Sarah knew. Which reminded her of her own possible pregnancy. Her heart fluttered at the thought that she might be going to become a mother, her hands lifting to press gently on her flat stomach.

'Are you already in there?' she whispered.

Sarah wasn't sure if she was still horrified at the thought, or secretly thrilled to pieces. She wanted to have a family, but only if she had the right man as the father; a man who loved her and trusted her. She'd thought that man would be Scott, and that any children they had would be conceived out of love, not some wild burst of black rage and jealousy.

One thing Sarah *was* sure of. When she rang Scott tonight—as she'd promised Cleo—there would be no mention of a possible pregnancy. Neither was she going to agree to go home to him. Hell, no. Sarah was also determined not to be alone with Scott till she knew for sure that he was the same man she'd first thought he was. Decent and strong and civilised, not the primitive caveman he'd become since getting those photos. She found that man way too intimidating, too dangerous, too perversely sexy. Not that she hadn't always found him sexy. Now, however, Sarah found herself quivering at the thought of having sex with him, her mind filling with erotic images that were primitive and wanton and way too disturbing.

'Oh, God,' she cried softly, and stumbled up the rest of the stairs.

CHAPTER NINE

SCOTT WAS SPRAWLED out on the chesterfield in his study, downing his third whisky, when his phone rang. Sighing—he despised talking on the phone—he extracted it from his trouser pocket, his rather sluggish heartbeat stopping altogether when he saw the identity of his caller. Sarah!

For a brief moment he contemplated not answering—what was good for the goose was good for the gander!—but he couldn't resist finding out what had made her change her mind and contact him before the stated fortnight was up. The thought that she might have finally realised how bloody-minded she was being did not ease his frustration as he lifted the phone to his ear.

'To what do I owe this honour?' he drawled caustically.

Sarah gritted her teeth. She'd known underneath this wasn't a good idea. She herself wasn't ready to talk to Scott, especially when he'd obviously been drinking. But a promise was a promise.

'I thought,' she said with much more politeness than she was feeling, 'that we might talk.'

'Really? So you finally believe me about that bastard, Leighton?'

'I haven't even spoken to Phil,' Sarah admitted.

'Why not?'

'I, um, didn't go to work this week.'

'Why not?' Definite surprise in his voice.

No way was she going to tell him the truth. 'I've had a sinus infection,' she said, choosing a problem she was susceptible to. Though usually not in the colder months. 'I should be ready to go back next Monday. But I doubt I'll be able to put my mind on the job till we sort things out between us. Which is why I think we should have a long talk this weekend.'

'I'm not much good at long talks,' he pointed out.

'True,' she agreed. Scott had always been a man of few words, the strong, silent type who didn't open his mouth except to give directions and make decisions. He wasn't interested in just talking for the sake of talking. Sarah herself wasn't a natural gossip or a chatterbox. Neither was she given to telling her life story at the drop of a hat as some females did. Cory had been the exception, perhaps because he had a highly empathetic nature. Even so, Cory didn't know absolutely *everything*. And Scott...well, he knew next to nothing, really. He was entirely ignorant of all the sordid little details of her ghastly home life.

It came to Sarah that she didn't know all that much about *his* upbringing, either. Which wasn't right. Even before Cleo had said so to her, she'd known that a married couple—especially ones who might be about to become parents—shouldn't have any secrets from each other. They should know each other like the backs of their hands. Sarah was forced to concede that if she'd told Scott the full truth about her father—not to mention her bastard of a brother—then he would have known instinctively that she'd *never* be unfaithful to him.

It was definitely high time to remedy that situation; time to do something constructive to save their marriage. Running away never solved anything. She'd done that after her mother had died and it hadn't achieved a single damned thing. Yes, she'd seen the world, but she hadn't really *seen* it for a long time, grief and depression dogging her footsteps. She probably should have stayed at home and had some counselling first. But then she would have missed her amazing experiences in Asia where she'd kept out of the large cities, staying in lots of small villages and living the simple life. Witnessing first-hand the love those families had for each other had been better than any counselling. What she wouldn't give to be back there now.

Sarah sighed. No point in thinking like that. Their world was not her world. Her world was Sydney and Scott and a marriage that was floundering.

Perhaps this time counselling might be some kind of answer.

'Look, I know you definitely don't like talking for long over the phone,' she said, 'so how about we meet somewhere for lunch tomorrow?' Sarah hoped that meeting with him in a public place would stop her from being distracted by the disturbing desires that being in his presence kept producing.

'Sorry. No can do. I'll be at Randwick races at lunchtime tomorrow. Have to present the trophy for the first race. It's the McAllister Mines Stakes. Why don't you come with me?'

Sarah was seriously tempted. She'd always loved going to the races with Scott, loved the vibrant atmosphere, loved looking at the horses, plus the way he always seemed to back the right horse to win. He was lucky like that. But whilst a racecourse offered her the safety of a public place, she wouldn't have the opportunity to have any kind of deep and meaningful conversation with Scott. He'd be constantly surrounded by officials and other owners and trainers, all trying to talk him into buying a horse, something he'd always vowed never to do, claiming that owning a racehorse was an even riskier investment than owning a mine.

As much as she still wanted to say yes, in the end Sarah decided against it.

'I'd rather not,' she said with some regret. 'How about dinner tomorrow night instead?'

'How about I come over to see you right now?' he counter-suggested.

Sarah sucked in sharply, hating the way her traitorous body leapt at this proposal.

'I don't think so, Scott,' she said stiffly. 'Could we just stick to dinner tomorrow night, please?'

His sigh was heavy. 'All right. Where?'

'It doesn't matter where. You choose. Preferably a place with plenty of room where we won't be squashed in like sardines.'

'I'll get us a table at that seafood restaurant you like down on the quay. I can never remember the name.'

'The Seafood Palace?'

'Yes. That's the one.'

'You'll be lucky to get a table there on a Saturday night.'

'I'll get a table, don't you worry. What time?'

'Eight?' she suggested. By then she'd be starving. *Though for what?* came the corrupting thought. Oh, hell…

'That's miles too late,' Scott said. 'Make it seven.'

Sarah resigned herself to a long and frustrating evening. 'All right. Seven.'

'I'll pick you up at a quarter to.'

Sarah winced. She didn't want to be alone in a car with him; didn't want him driving her home afterwards. But she knew she was being silly. This was about them trying to smooth things out—pouncing on her in the car was not Scott's style. 'Very well. Pick me up, then.'

'Good,' he said. 'It's good to see you letting go of some of that stubbornness, Sarah. See you tomorrow,' he said and then hung up on her.

His rudeness startled her at first, and Sarah sniffed haughtily as she whirled and stalked into the guest bedroom where her eyes lit on the pregnancy testing kit sitting on the bedside table.

'I am *not* stubborn,' she muttered under her breath. 'I am, however, possibly pregnant.'

She picked up the kit and carried it into the bathroom where she opened it and read through the full instructions, tempted beyond bearing to take the test. Common sense kept telling her that it was still too soon for the test to be reliable, and that nothing was to be gained by getting a false negative. Nothing but false comfort. In the end, common sense won, Sarah shoving everything back in the box, unused, and marching out of the bathroom, leaving the damned thing behind.

But the thought of her possible pregnancy haunted her for hours that night. What would Scott say if she *was* pregnant? Would he be pleased, seeing it as the means to mend their marriage? Or would he be suspicious and accuse her of infidelity again?

Of course, suspicion over the identity of the father didn't cut it these days, Sarah conceded, a simple DNA test always putting the matter to rest. But she would hate to see initial scepticism in Scott's eyes. She was right when she said that this ultimate form of distrust would be the kiss of death where their marriage was concerned. But perhaps she was putting the cart before the horse. Maybe there wouldn't be any baby.

But feminine instinct whispered to her that there was. Sarah didn't fall asleep till the early hours of the morning.

CHAPTER TEN

SARAH SIGHED AS she looked at the pile of clothes scattered over the bed. Truly, she was acting like some teenager going on her first date, trying on and discarding practically everything in her wardrobe.

'It's all Cory's fault,' she muttered as she started hanging some of them back up again. They'd had a brief text exchange this morning where she'd confessed she was going to dinner with Scott tonight and he'd replied that it was a good idea and she was to wear something extra sexy.

Stupid advice, given she was trying to resist the temptation to have any further sex with Scott. If she dressed extra sexy it would definitely send out the opposite message to him.

Still, whilst dressing *extra* sexy was out, Sarah found herself wanting to at least look sort of sexy.

The trouble was Sarah didn't dress even sort of sexy. Not the way some women did. She didn't wear low-cut tops or too tight, too short skirts. Her choice of wardrobe was very elegant and feminine, flattering but never provocative, her mother having shown her how to choose colours and clothes that complemented her fair hair and willowy figure. Sarah never dressed in anything too dark or too bright. At work, she combined cream or taupe suits with soft silky blouses in pastels or delicate florals. Her skirts, whilst nicely fitted, were kept to knee length, and she always—always—wore stockings, expensive stockings that had a faint sheen and drew the eye to her shapely calves and slender ankles. She also always chose shoes and a bag in a nude colour, which went with everything. For after-work wear she usually wore dressy dresses, several of which would have done for dinner tonight.

But Sarah wasn't happy with any of them, finally settling on a pair of champagne-coloured crepe trousers that had a matching jacket, which she'd bought two years ago and which occasionally made an appearance during the cooler months. It was the middle of May, and Sydney's Indian summer was definitely on the wane. This evening was sure to be quite cool. Of course, the restaurant would be heated so she needed to wear something nice underneath in case she had to take off her jacket. Sarah had an awful feeling that she might be feeling hot around Scott.

A rather erotic shiver rippled down her spine at this last thought. Oh, Lord!

Finding the right top proved surprisingly difficult. She discarded her usual choices. Wearing a cami was just too bare. In the end, she chose a gold beaded top, which she'd bought on sale and never worn. Admittedly, it was still sleeveless but it had a scooped neckline that wasn't too low.

Sarah finished off the outfit with nude high heels, a gold clutch purse and gold jewellery. Nothing too much. Just a slim chain around her neck, which had belonged to her mother, and some small gold ear studs she'd bought for herself overseas. None of the jewellery Scott had bought for her. Not that there was all that much. He wasn't a gift giver in the main. Though he did present her with some lovely cultured pearls on their wedding day and a diamond pendant with matching earrings on her birthday last November. For Christmas he'd bought her the red car.

By six thirty-five Sarah was dressed and fully made up, but still she dithered. Maybe she shouldn't wear her hair down. Scott *loved* her hair down. It had been down on the day they'd first met. Maybe she should put it up. Tightly up. No, she didn't have the time to do that. She compromised by putting it up at the sides, using two pearl-encrusted combs that were pretty and feminine and which she often wore to work. Not on that fateful day fifteen months ago, however. That day, her hair had been fully out, falling in a sleek creamy curtain over her shoulders and halfway down her back. Since then, she'd had it cut a bit. Now, it stopped just short of her shoulder blades. But it was still her crowning glory. Or so her mother used to say.

Thinking of her mother did Sarah the world of good. Because it reminded her why she had to resist Scott's sex appeal tonight and concentrate on fixing their relationship. Or try to. Which meant having some long discussions over dinner, telling him all the things she'd never told him before, then finding out his own deep dark secrets. He was sure to have some. Everyone did, didn't they?

Just before a quarter to seven, Sarah picked up her purse and started making her way downstairs. The doorbell rang before she reached the bottom step, her heart jolting to a stop before lurching into an agitated rhythm. Scooping in a huge lungful of air, she let it out slowly then forced herself to keep going, lecturing herself all the while.

Play it cool, girl. Cool and calm. Tap into some of that natural poise people keep saying you've got. Don't, for pity's sake, start going ga-ga over the man, no matter how good he looks or how sexy you find him.

The lecture worked well till she opened the door and saw Scott standing there, dressed in the sort of clothes that added to his macho appeal. Dark jeans, an opened-neck white shirt, covered by a smart jacket. It wasn't an outfit she had chosen for him, or that she'd ever seen in his wardrobe. Clearly, he'd been out clothes shopping, wanting to wear something new for her. Maybe it felt like a first date to him as well.

'Looking good, Scott,' she complimented, doing her level best to ignore the fluttering in her stomach.

'Not as good as you,' he returned, his gaze hot and hungry as it roved over her.

Sarah scooped in another gathering breath. 'What? This old thing?' she tossed off nonchalantly.

His smile almost undid her feigned cool. God, but it was a sexy smile. Not all teeth. Just a wry lifting at the corners of his mouth and a knowing light in his glittering grey eyes. 'I haven't seen that top before,' he said. 'Anyway, you look fabulous. But then, you always look fabulous.'

'Wow. Flattery, Scott? That's not like you.'

'I'm a desperate man tonight. Come on. Let's get going.'

'I have to lock up first.'

'Cory not home?' he asked whilst she did so.

Sarah noted an oddly knowing note in the question, the reason for which eluded her. Perhaps he'd noticed that Cory's car wasn't parked in the street. Not many terraced houses in Paddington had off-street parking.

'On a Saturday night?' she hedged. 'You have to be joking. Where's *your* car?' she added as she glanced up and down the street.

'Just round the corner. This is a dreadful street to park in at the weekends.'

'I should have taken a taxi to the restaurant,' she told him as they walked along together.

'That's not what I wanted,' Scott returned, his hands slipping into his pockets. 'You don't get to hold all the cards in this, Sarah. You have to consider my wishes as well if you want us to get back together.'

When she stopped and gaped over at him, Scott laughed. 'You should see the look on your face. Truly, Sarah darling, a lawyer should never forget that there are always two sides to a story. I might have done the wrong thing last Friday night, but you haven't exactly played nice this past week.'

Sarah had always found personal criticism a hard pill to swallow, especially one that rang true. She'd been so busy feeling sorry for herself that she hadn't really stopped to think how those photos had affected Scott. Even when Cleo had come over last night and pointed out how much he was hurting, she hadn't really taken it on board. Scott's comment now hit home, making her feel terrible.

'You're right,' she said. 'I haven't. And I'm sorry.'

'No need to apologise. Look, I can admit when I'm in the wrong and I behaved badly last week. I wish I could turn back the clock. But perhaps you overreacted a little too? If you'd just stayed, we could have eventually sorted everything out. Instead, we've both ended up being miserable and lonely all week.'

Sarah refused to let him whitewash what he'd done. Or put the blame on her. Her father used to do that with her mother, tell her she was overreacting and that it was all her fault if he looked at other women. Which was what he used to claim in the beginning. That he was just *looking*. And her poor silly mother had swallowed that. For a while…

Sarah had no intention of backing down. 'I don't agree with that at all, Scott,' she replied. 'Nothing would have been sorted out if I'd stayed. What happened last weekend showed we have some deep-seated problems in our relationship.'

'Would you care to elaborate on that?'

'I will when we get to the restaurant—did you manage to get us a table at the Seafood Palace?'

'I did. Money talks all languages. It gets men like me the most beautiful wives and the best of tables.'

Sarah stared up at him. 'You still think I married you for your money?' she asked, startled.

Scott just shrugged. 'To be honest, Sarah, I have no idea why you married me.'

'I married you because I loved you,' Sarah answered, feeling quite angry with him for doubting her motives. But it put a different perspective on why he might have believed her unfaithful to him. 'I've always wanted you,' she added, anxious now to convince him. 'Right from the first moment I set eyes on you.'

'That's another thing which bothers me,' he ground out. 'You were a virgin when we met. It doesn't make sense that you lusted after me the way you seemed to but not any other man before me. It's not like you wouldn't have been pursued by the opposite sex before, Sarah. You are one hot-looking babe.'

Sarah winced, then sighed. She should have told Scott the truth about her upbringing from the word go. Then he would understand why she'd been so wary of men for most of her life. She vowed then and there to do what Cleo had suggested last night. Tell Scott everything.

Well…perhaps not *everything*! She wasn't about to mention her pregnancy scare till everything had been sorted out to her satisfaction. Why make more trouble, if there was no need?

'I understand your confusion,' she told him with utmost sincerity. 'But there are reasons why I was still a virgin when I met you, reasons which will take a while to explain. Could we wait till we get to the restaurant? Then I'll answer all your questions. And you can answer some of mine,' she finished up firmly, determined not to lose control of tonight's conversation.

CHAPTER ELEVEN

THE SEAFOOD PALACE was five star plus, from its top-class menu to its setting overlooking Sydney harbour. The dining room was spacious, with the tables not too close together, each one covered in a crisp white linen cloth and set with the best of cutlery and glasses. In the centre was a small crystal candlestick—complete with a not-too-high candle—which the *maître d'* lit with a flourish after he showed them to their set-for-two table. Undoubtedly it was the best and most romantic spot in the house, situated in a semi-circular alcove that had a huge bay window, affording its privileged diners a magnificent view of the water and the nearby Harbour Bridge.

'Andre will be your waiter for tonight,' the suave *maître d'* informed them as he held out the chair for Sarah. 'Enjoy,' he added, flashing Scott a wide smile before leaving them in the hands of the eager-faced young man.

And well he might smile, Scott thought wryly, given the tip he'd promised the man for securing him this table on such short notice. At the time, Scott's only intention for tonight was to impress the pants off Sarah—quite literally. He'd honestly thought he could get her back via the mutual chemistry that still sizzled between them. That was why he'd left the races as soon as he could today and gone clothes shopping, determined to show up looking his best. He'd thought his plan had worked when she'd opened the door and practically drooled. But somehow things had become sidetracked during their walk to the car. Her stating that she should have taken a taxi had annoyed him, and soon he'd been saying things to her that would have been better left unsaid. But the damage was done now, and, if he was brutally honest, he did want answers to the questions he'd posed.

Meanwhile, perhaps it would be a good idea to soften her up with some champagne. Sarah liked good champagne. But when he asked her if she wanted a bottle or just a glass, she disappointed him by declining altogether, saying she was sorry but she wasn't allowed to drink alcohol whilst taking the antibiotics for her sinus.

'Just some sparkling mineral water for me,' she said, smiling up at their waiter.

Talk about the best-laid plans of mice and men, Scott thought frustratedly.

'In that case bring me a beer,' he added, feeling quite put out.

'What kind, sir?'

'Any of the pale ales will do.'

Sarah hated lying to Scott but what else could she do? She had to give him some reason for turning down her favourite drink. It wasn't the right time to tell him that she'd forgotten to take her pill for some time and now she might be pregnant. But only *might*. Tonight was supposed to be about the past, not an unproven future. Sarah picked up the menu and started studying it, suddenly aware that she didn't have much of an appetite. Nerves gathered in her stomach at the thought of telling Scott the unvarnished truth about her totally dysfunctional and somewhat sordid family life.

'You order for me, will you?' she asked him, and put down the menu. 'I always like what you order more than what I order, anyway.'

'True,' he replied with a rueful smile. 'You can be indecisive at times.'

'Not something anyone would ever accuse you of being,' she countered with a dry laugh.

'I usually know what I want,' he told her, his eyes colliding with hers across the table.

And there it was, the same hunger Sarah had glimpsed in those glittering grey depths on the first day they'd met. This time, however, she refused to surrender to its primal pull. She would not let him seduce her tonight. No way! She'd come here to talk to him. Nothing else.

Still, it took a real effort to drag her eyes away from his and pretend to inspect the view.

'It's a very pretty spot here at night, isn't it?' she said, striving for a casual tone.

'Very,' he agreed in an annoyingly smug voice. It came to her that he honestly expected her to come home later tonight. It also came to her that behind her steadfast resolve to resist him lay the wickedest of temptations. *It wouldn't hurt to go to bed with him, would it? At least you might sleep tonight for a change.*

By the time her eyes returned to his, she wasn't

so sure that she would say no to him, underlining his accusation of her being indecisive at times. Perhaps if she started talking about all those things she hated talking about, she would stop being turned on. Nothing guaranteed to make her feel cold inside more than remembering the life she'd led at home.

But before she could launch into her sorry tale, Andre returned with their drinks, Scott grabbing the opportunity to order at the same time, choosing fresh rock oysters for their entrées, grilled barramundi in a lemon and parsley sauce for the main, along with salad side dishes, finishing up with the most decadent-sounding chocolate cheesecake for dessert.

'With ice cream, not cream,' he added.

'You do love your ice cream,' she said after the waiter departed.

Sarah realised she already knew a little more about Scott's upbringing than he did about hers. She knew his mother had died when he was very young and he'd been brought up by his father, who'd been a less than successful prospector. Intelligent, though, having a degree in geology. He'd home-schooled Scott, home being a Kombi-van in which they'd traversed every state in Australia, looking for that pot of gold. His dad had occasionally made a killing, finding a few valuable opals at Lightning Ridge, plus a couple of decent-sized gold nuggets, their proceeds funding the purchase of those parcels of land that had eventually proved to contain true treasure. Whenever money ran seriously low, his father would get work in one of the coal mines and they'd live in a local caravan park, where Scott ran wild and free.

'That was the life,' he'd told her once.

Thinking about that now, she rather agreed. Anything would have been better than her own stressed and distressed existence.

'Time for you to do that explaining, Sarah,' Scott said, breaking the rather tense silence that had enveloped the table. 'We're alone, so no more excuses, please.'

Sarah picked up her mineral water and took a sip before speaking. Her mouth had dried, her throat thickening with her memories. When you'd never really told anyone the total truth about something it was very difficult to know even where to begin.

'My father didn't just have one affair,' she blurted out. 'He was a serial cheater for as long as I can remember.'

Scott didn't seem shocked, though his expression was thoughtful.

'He never bothered to hide his dalliances,' Sarah swept on. 'Sometimes he would go off with some woman for the whole weekend. It used to drive Mum mad. The rows they had were monumental.'

Now Scott was frowning. 'Why didn't she just leave him?'

Sarah laughed. It was not a happy laugh. 'I used to say exactly the same thing. Lots of times. But no,' Sarah added after another sip of mineral water, 'she always took him back. She said it was because she loved him. And maybe she did, in her own masochistic way. She would never have divorced him if he hadn't left her first. For a younger, but very wealthy woman, by the way.'

'I see. What did your father do for a crust?'

'He used to sell quality cars. You know. Ferraris

and Porsches and cars like that. He was a good sales-
man, too. Made an excellent living. We never wanted
for anything, financially, not even after the divorce.
Dad gave Mum the family home and paid for my
education so I can't complain about that.'

'It sounds like your life was better after the divorce,' Scott pointed out.

'Oh, it was, for a while. It was a relief to have Dad
out of the house. But an even bigger relief to never
have to see my bastard brother ever again!'

CHAPTER TWELVE

THE ARRIVAL OF their oysters interrupted Sarah's story at this startling statement, Scott wondering what her brother had done to make her talk about him like that. Something not very nice, he was sure. Her face had twisted with the memory, her eyes filling with distaste.

'What did he do to make you so mad with him?' he asked quietly after the waiter left.

'Victor. His name was Victor. Lord, what *didn't* he do? The creep. He was five years older than me and by the time I turned thirteen he was eighteen. And a total sex addict. Watched porn on his computer all the time. Treated his multiple girlfriends like crap. Cheated on all of them. Like father like son, I guess.'

'He didn't try anything with you, did he?' Scott said, worried now.

'No, but he enjoyed using his power to scare me into thinking he would. He'd threaten me and generally made my life hell every way he could think of. When he started *accidentally* coming into the bathroom we shared when I was in there, I went and bought a bolt so that I could lock it from the inside.'

Scott swore and another deep shudder ran through her.

'That's terrible, Sarah,' Scott said, beginning to understand why she'd stayed a virgin for a long time. 'But not all men are like that,' he added gently.

'I know,' she said, and smiled at him. 'But it took me a long time to trust one again. I just didn't like them. Or trust them. Even when I first went to university, I was still wary. Whenever a male student took an interest in me, I blew them off, quick smart. Then Mum died and I think I must have had some kind of breakdown.' She gave him a guilty look, then. 'Her death wasn't an accidental overdose like I told you. It was suicide.'

When tears pricked at her eyes, Scott decided enough was enough. Any more soul-shattering stories could wait till later, when she was safely in his arms and he could comfort her properly.

'I think, my darling,' he said with a warm smile, 'that you should stop talking about upsetting subjects for now and just concentrate on eating these truly delicious oysters. I am no longer curious over why you were still a virgin when we met. And I can see how your being an unfaithful wife would be the last thing you would ever do. I'm just sorry I ever pushed the issue in the first place. So let's forget about distressing confessions for now… If I'd known what you went through…'

'I want to be honest with you,' Sarah replied as she stabbed one of the oysters with her fork. 'And for you to be honest with me. If our marriage is to survive, we can't keep secrets from each other.' Especially big ones like she'd forgotten the pill and just might be pregnant.

Sarah opened her mouth to confess but the words simply wouldn't come, her panicky mind finding all sorts of excuses not to tell him, the main one being she might not be pregnant at all! Why risk more trouble? Far better to wait till she was sure that Scott really did love and trust her before hitting their fragile marriage with added stress.

And a baby was definitely added stress.

Meanwhile, everything else had to be aired. Like her private financial stash. She hoped it wouldn't make him angry that she'd kept that a secret.

'There's one more thing I must tell you,' she said.

Scott looked alarmed.

'No, nothing too dreadful,' she hurried on. 'It's just that I inherited a substantial amount when Mum died. The house for starters—which I sold—and quite a bit of cash. So I definitely didn't marry you for your money,' she told him with a touch of acerbity, having been cut that he'd even thought for a moment that she might be a gold-digger. 'I have plenty of my own. Though not enough, unfortunately, to bail out that refinery of yours. From what I gathered, that's going to take millions.'

'You're right about that,' Scott said ruefully.

'You're welcome to what I've got,' she offered rather impulsively.

'Thanks, but no thanks. You might need it one day, the way the mining industry is going.'

'You're not really in deep financial trouble, are you, Scott? I mean, I wouldn't have suggested this restaurant if I thought you were going broke.'

'Don't trouble your pretty little head about that. I'm not an idiot. I have plenty of assets and a steady private income from other sources. I have more than enough to pay the bill. And to support a wife. When and if she ever comes home... I nearly went insane this last week. I miss you, Sarah. I want you to come home.'

Sarah sighed. Trust him to use this opportunity to bring that matter up. This was why she hadn't wanted to see him in the first place. That, and the uncontrollable lust he kept evoking in her. She missed him too. Or she missed his body. *That* was what seemed to be uppermost in her mind at the moment. Oh, God, everything was such a mess. 'I...I'll think about it,' she said. 'Now let's just eat our food.'

They ate the oysters in silence, Scott clearly not happy with her decision. Or her lack of it. When the waiter came to clear their plates, he ordered another beer for himself and a second mineral water for her.

'For a girl who wanted to talk,' he said after the waiter departed, 'you've gone quiet all of a sudden.'

If he knew the reason behind her fraught silence, she'd be in big trouble. With great difficulty, she refocused her heated brain on why she'd agreed to this dinner date in the first place. Unfortunately, this meant she had to look across the table at Scott, and into those sexy eyes of his. Her casual shrug was a sham. There was nothing casual going on inside Sarah.

'I guess I've told you everything I wanted to tell you,' she said, doing her best to stay calm. 'I needed you to understand what has made me the way I am. Why I react to things the way I do. If we'd talked more before we married, things might not have gone so wrong last Friday. You would have trusted me more. You would have known that it would have been impossible for me to be an unfaithful wife.'

'Yeah, you're probably right. I rushed you to the altar. But damn it all, Sarah, I don't regret it. I do regret not trusting you and I regret what I did last Friday night. But you have to admit, what we did, it was pretty amazing. You were something that night! I'm crazy about that girl and I want more of her.'

Sarah felt his hunger right through every pore in her body. Felt her own desire too, from the tips of her erect nipples right down to the melting heat between her thighs. Thank God the waiter arrived back with their drinks, breaking the dangerous moment and letting her have a breather.

'Well, I'm not so crazy about that girl, Scott,' she managed to say once they were alone. 'She's way too much of a pushover for my liking. Now could we kindly get back to discussing things that really matter?'

'Like what?'

'Like why *did* you rush me to the altar? Why did you marry me at all?'

CHAPTER THIRTEEN

SCOTT WAS SO taken aback by her questions that he was speechless for a few seconds.

'Well?' Sarah prompted.

He finally found his tongue. 'You know very well why I married you,' he threw back at her. 'I was madly in love with you, woman. Trust me when I say it wasn't just a matter of lust. I know how lust feels and that wasn't what I felt for you.' He'd fallen madly in love with her. Absolutely. But what he'd also felt was fear. Fear that he'd somehow lose this incredibly beautiful, bright creature if he didn't marry her quick smart; that if he didn't put his ring on her finger then one day soon some other better-looking, more charming, more sophisticated man would come along and win her away from him. He couldn't risk that so, yes, he'd rushed her to the altar whilst she was still as bewitched with him as he was with her.

But ultimately, it hadn't worked, had it? That man he'd feared had come along, and even if Sarah hadn't fallen into his arms, *he'd* believed she had. And in doing so, he'd risked the one thing he feared most of all. Losing Sarah.

But you haven't lost her yet, you fool, whispered the voice of reason. *Use your brains, man.*

Scott knew women liked to talk, but it hadn't been a big part of his upbringing. His father only opened his mouth to show him something or impart knowledge. Scott only knew a handful of details about his father's past life, and quite frankly this hadn't bothered him, but it seemed women just had to know everything about everyone. Scott had learned this over time. He'd had girlfriends before Sarah. But confiding didn't come naturally to him and Sarah had seemed to understand this. In the beginning, that was. Clearly, she no longer liked his close-mouthed reticence. It was time to talk about the one subject he hated talking about. The past.

But first he had to answer her question over why he'd rushed her to the altar.

'If you want me to be brutally honest,' he began, 'I married you because I wanted to have you all to myself, twenty-four-seven. I didn't know the reason then for your wariness about the opposite sex, but I could see you weren't the sort of girl who'd live with me, or become my mistress. So marriage seemed the only course of action, and the sooner the better. Like I said, I was crazy about you, Sarah. I'd never felt anything even close before to what I felt for you. To be totally honest with you I wasn't too fond of women for a good while after I found out the ugly truth about my mother.'

'*Your* mother?' Sarah queried, startled.

'Yes. You see, she didn't die when I was a baby. That's just a lie I tell to hide the truth.'

Sarah sat up straighter in her chair, stunned by this highly unexpected revelation.

'She also wasn't married to my father,' Scott went on. 'She was a good-time girl Dad picked up when he struck gold once. Their fling finished once the money ran out and Dad took off again for the outback. He didn't realise at the time that he'd left behind a piece of himself. Anyway, to cut a long story short, a couple of years later, when he was flushed with finding some black opals, he looked her up again. She was living on some kind of hippie commune by then, up near one of the Northern NSW beaches. Imagine his surprise when he came across a little toddler who was the spitting image of him, running around the front yard, stark naked, whilst she was inside totally out of it in a pot-smoking haze.'

'Good Lord! What did he do?'

'Paid her some money and took me away with him.'

'Didn't she fight him for you?' Sarah couldn't imagine any mother letting her child go that easily. She certainly wouldn't have. She'd have created bloody hell!

'No. She told Dad he was welcome to me—that I was an uncontrollable brat and she'd never wanted me anyway.'

'Oh, Scott,' Sarah said sadly, her heart going out to him.

'No need to feel sorry for me,' he said matter-of-factly. 'I don't remember her or miss her. And Dad was a great dad. A little unconventional but he loved me to death and I felt the same way about him. He didn't tell me the truth about my mother till I was a grown man and could take it.'

Sarah blinked back her tears but didn't say a word.

'I did look my mother up a few years ago,' Scott went on, 'more out of curiosity then need. But she'd died a decade or so earlier. Too many drugs, I guess. The funny thing was this old junkie who'd known her said she was never the same after Dad took me away. That all the life went out of her. So maybe she sort of loved me after all.'

'I'm sure she did,' Sarah said soothingly.

Scott wasn't sure of any such thing. Women liked to romanticise situations, he'd found. Still, perhaps it was a nice thought, but not one that he wished to dwell on.

'Enough of this,' he said a bit sharply. 'I've never seen the point of rehashing old hurts. Let's just concentrate on the here and now, which is enjoying each other's company, and our next course.' Which he spotted being brought to the table.

They did enjoy the barramundi. Sort of. Sarah's mood remained a little sad, however, Scott frustrated that she refused to have even one glass of wine with the main course. He knew the directions always said you couldn't drink alcohol with antibiotics, but surely one glass wouldn't hurt. It might relax her; put some joy back into her.

Of course, there was another way to relax her…

'I think we might skip dessert,' he said, glancing across the table at her, his eyes glittering as he made his meaning clear.

CHAPTER FOURTEEN

SARAH TRIED NOT to blush. But it was no use. The image of Scott doing wicked things to her sent heat zooming up from her chest to her neck and into her face. Her throat was parched as her heartbeat quickened.

'Are you trying to turn me on, Scott?'

'Am I succeeding? Be honest now.'

'Yes,' she choked out.

'Let's go, then.'

'I am not going back to our apartment with you, Scott. Not yet.'

'I didn't ask you to. Cory's place will do just as well for tonight.'

Sarah knew she was fighting a losing battle but she refused to relent easily. 'Cory might have brought someone home by now,' she said in a desperate defence.

'Not very likely. He's at a conference in Melbourne.'

Sarah gasped. 'How did you know that?'

'He texted me this afternoon and told me so, something which seemed to slip your mind, Miss Honesty.'

Sarah gritted her teeth. 'I'm going to kill him.'

'I wanted to kiss him.'

'Oh, really?' she said archly. 'I didn't think you cared for him in that way.'

He grinned. 'Neither did I. Maybe it has something to do with my wife neglecting her marital duties this past week.'

Sarah rolled her eyes at the cheek of him. But it was no use. A smile grabbed her mouth and soon she was laughing. 'What chance did I have, with you two conspiring against me?'

'No chance at all. I'll just get the bill and we'll go.'

'I need to visit the powder room first.'

Scott scowled gently. 'Is this another delaying tactic? You won't make a dash for it out of the back window, will you?'

'Maybe I should.' And she meant it. For nothing would be solved by going to bed with Scott. They still had a lot of talking to do, on both sides.

But the compelling nature of her desires would not be denied. Sarah wanted Scott to make love to her tonight, all night. And maybe all tomorrow. She wanted him to take her to that hot, heady place again where logical thinking ceased and the only thing she cared about was her next orgasm, along with all the wild dizzying pleasure in between. That was where she'd been that fateful Friday night. And she wanted to experience that again.

Her legs almost didn't support her when she rose and made her way unsteadily to the powder room. As she washed her hands she didn't dare look at her reflection in the wall mirror, afraid of what she might see. Her mother perhaps, that poor tragic creature whom Sarah physically resembled but who didn't have one ounce of willpower when it came to her husband.

I will not be like that, Sarah vowed as she left the room. *I will not!*

Scott was waiting for her, the bill paid, wasting no time ushering her outside and into the small car park set aside for patrons of the restaurant. The touch of his hand in the small of her back sent little shivers running up and down her spine. They didn't speak during the short drive home, Sarah not even glancing over at him. She didn't want to see smugness in his face, or desire. She had enough to contend with trying to handle her own.

This time, Scott was able to park close to Cory's house, some of the other inhabitants of the street obviously having gone out.

'It's a bit chilly in here,' he said once they entered the hallway.

'Cory hasn't installed heating or air-conditioning yet,' Sarah told him. 'It's to go in with the renovations. But that's been delayed. There's a great little heater in here though,' she said, leading Scott into the downstairs living room.

'And a great big sofa,' he added, turning her in his arms and kissing her before she could do a single thing. Not a slow, tender, loving kiss. A hard, hot, hungry kiss, which echoed the frustration both of them had been feeling all week. She accepted his tongue avidly, sucking on it as she wanted to suck on *him*. When he wrenched his head away she moaned in protest.

'Don't worry,' he growled. 'I feel exactly the same way.'

Sarah extricated herself from his grip to turn on

the heater and take some of the cushions from the sofa
and throw them on top of the thick shag rug that lay
in front of the heater. Because no way was she going
to have sex with Scott on that lounge like a pair of
horny teenagers.

'Good thinking,' he said, tossing aside his jacket
before pulling her into his arms again.

Another savage kiss completely obliterated any lin-
gering doubt Sarah might have had about doing this,
confirming in her mind this was what *she* wanted.
There was no question of being seduced, or in any
way coerced.

'Too many clothes, sweetheart,' he muttered when
his head finally lifted.

'Yes,' she agreed throatily, her hands going to the
buttons on his shirt.

He laughed and just yanked the shirt off over his
head, exposing his magnificent chest to her touch.

And touch him she did, her fingernails scraping
over his skin as they slid through the sexy matt of
curls that covered the middle of his chest. When they
moved over his nipples, he groaned a raw animal
groan. When she did it again, his hands lifted to grip
her wrists.

'Best stop that,' he muttered. 'It's doing dreadful
things to me.'

'Good,' she said, and bent her lips to them instead.

'You've turned into a witch,' he growled. 'But I
love it.'

She lifted her head, determined not to let him think
she was his again, just because she desired him. 'This
isn't love, Scott. This is just lust.'

'That's a matter of opinion, sweetheart. But if you

want total honesty, then right now I don't give a damn what it is. I want you as I've never wanted you before, and if I don't have you in the next twenty seconds, I think I'm going to explode.'

Without further discussion and with little finesse he stripped her of her clothes then spread her out on the rug, ogling her naked body whilst he took off the rest of his own clothes, at which point it was Sarah's turn to do the ogling.

Scott was all man, she thought breathlessly. Big and strong, with a body that was as powerful as it was intimidating. She stared at the size of his erection and wondered how it ever fitted inside her. But it always did. Beautifully. Wondrously. Bringing her pleasure without even having to move.

But when it did...

He lay down and surged into her without preamble, the way he'd done the other day. Everything happened just as quickly as then too, both of them climaxing in no time, shuddering and shaking with the intensity of their rapid releases.

'Geez, Sarah,' Scott groaned as he collapsed across her, his weight making *her* groan in protest. He quickly rolled off her, Sarah gasping with relief.

'Sorry,' he said from where he lay beside her, his breathing still ragged. 'Didn't mean to squash you. When I've got my breath back we'll go have a shower together and I'll show you some more interesting moves.'

'More interesting?' she echoed, trying not to sound as instantly excited as she was.

'That's what you want, isn't it? Or would you prefer we do it the way we used to do it? Under the bed-covers with the lights off.'

Sarah winced. Surely she hadn't been as boring as that, had she?

Not quite, she conceded, but things sure hadn't been as adventurous as this. She'd never said no to Scott when it came to sex, but she'd been a passive partner, possibly because her lack of experience made her feel less confident. She'd always left everything up to Scott. Maybe he thought she was too shy for more adventurous activities. Just thinking of stand-ing up naked in a shower with him and having him wash her all over was doing her head in. Not in a bad way, either.

She looked over at him and he smiled.

'I love it when your eyes go all smoky like that. I know you were angry with me for last Friday night, but the sex was great, wasn't it? *You* were great. A bit naughty. But hot as hell.'

'*You* were the one who was naughty,' she pointed out, desperate to stop her mind from unravelling with desire.

He laughed. 'Oh, sweetheart, you are such an in-nocent! But that's what makes you so attractive to me. And why I fell in love with you. Because you were different from all the other women I've ever dated, none of whom I ever wanted to marry.'

Sarah levered herself up on one elbow to stare down at him. 'Are you saying you married me be-cause I was a virgin when we met?'

'Partly. But I also wanted to be in a position to protect you.'

'*Protect* me?'

'Sure. A woman of your obvious attractions needs protection from the big bad wolves in this world.'

Sarah had to admit that when she was with Scott, she did feel safe and secure. Till recently…

'Too much talking,' Scott said, and abruptly sat up. 'Come on. Let's go shower.'

CHAPTER FIFTEEN

SARAH SHIVERED AS Scott led her from the warm living room, down the cold hallway and into the rather ancient bathroom that hadn't been updated in years. It was very clean, though, Cory meticulous when it came to housework. There was a small strip heater on the wall, which Scott immediately turned on, followed by the taps in the shower.

'Not exactly built for two, is it?' Scott said drily as they waited for the water to get hot enough.

'At least it d-doesn't have a shower c-curtain,' she stammered, her teeth beginning to chatter.

Scott gave her a droll look whilst he rubbed her goosebumped upper arms with his large hands. 'Just think. We could be at home right now, with ducted air-conditioning and a huge two-headed shower stall.'

'Don't tempt me,' she replied.

'Could I?'

'No.'

'We'll see, Miss Stubborn. We'll see.'

Scott loved the way her lovely blue eyes widened, then glittered with an intoxicating mixture of shock and excitement. This new sexy Sarah bewitched him

even more than the shy virgin, because she promised
a lifetime of erotic pleasure with her as his wife. He
refused to believe that she had any intention of actually leaving him…that she would let one rotten mis-
understanding ruin their relationship. Yes, he'd hurt
her badly by not trusting her. He could see that now.
But surely she would forgive him. She wouldn't have
come to dinner tonight at all if she hadn't been having second thoughts about her actions. Neither would
she have let him have sex with her if she didn't still
love him. Sarah thought it was lust driving her but
he knew differently. It was love. It had always been
love. He was sure of it, he thought as he followed her
under the jets of hot water, resolving to leave no stone
unturned in seducing the woman he loved into coming back home with him.

It was a snug fit all right, Sarah conceded once Scott
slid the shower screen shut behind them. There was
nowhere to escape the streams of water beating down
over her head, plastering her hair to her skull and
back. There was hardly room to lift her arms to scoop
the wet locks back from her face.

'Oh!' she gasped when he turned her round and she
felt his erection pressing against her bottom.

'Hand me that soap there,' he ordered roughly.

Her hand trembled as she picked the cake of soap
up off the inbuilt soap dish, not sure what he intended
to do, not sure now if she was capable of stopping
him. Sarah might be a relative innocent when it came
to sexual experience but she wasn't ignorant.

She gasped again when he began rubbing the now
wet soap over her nipples. Lord, but it felt fantastic!

Her heart started galloping and she had the devil of a time stopping herself from moaning with pleasure. In the end she did.

'You like that?' he rasped in her ear.

'Mmm...' was all she could manage in reply.

'Sorry, sweetheart, but it's time to move on.'

When he slid the soap down over her stomach, Sarah sucked in sharply, fearful that if he rubbed that soap over her more intimate parts she would come straight away. But amazingly she didn't, Scott skilfully avoiding her clitoris and concentrating on the less sensitive areas. But she still became terribly tense, every muscle she owned tightening in anticipation.

'Dear God,' she choked out at one stage.

'Prayer won't help you tonight, sweetheart,' Scott warned her, then abruptly turned her round. 'Now do the same to me,' he ordered as he handed her the soap then leant back against the tiled wall, giving her enough room to follow his command.

Sarah didn't dare disobey him this time. Hell, she didn't *want* to disobey.

She echoed everything he'd done to her, rubbing the soap over his chest, concentrating on his nipples. Though smaller than hers, they were fiercely erect and just as sensitive, by the sounds he started making: low, raw groans that she found deliciously arousing, making her want to hear more. And more.

Her hand dropped away from his chest, drifting down over his rock-hard abs to the tip of his erection. When she brushed the cake of slippery soap over it, he swore, then grabbed her hand, stopping her from going further.

'No?' she enquired mischievously, her eyes as excited as his.

'No,' he growled, switching off the taps and slamming back the shower screen so hard that it rattled.

'But I *wanted* to,' she protested even as he reached for the towels.

'I wanted you to do it too,' he told her, shoving one towel into her hands whilst he kept the other. 'But I have other plans for you right now.'

Sarah trembled, her head spinning with desire.

His smile was so sexy. 'Shall we go?'

The downstairs living room was nicely warm when they returned, Scott wasting no time pulling her down onto the rug with him.

For a big man Scott was a quick mover. Before Sarah could blink he slid down her body and put his mouth where the cake of soap had recently been. She cried out when his lips took a rather ruthless possession of her swollen clitoris, sucking the electrified tip till it was impossible for her to stop herself from coming. This time her cries carried a degree of exasperation. She hadn't wanted to come; hadn't wanted the edge to be taken off her desires.

But strangely, that didn't happen. Yes, for a few moments she experienced a wave of post-orgasmic languor, but Scott put a stop to that when he slid back up her body and started kissing her nipples. That woke her up again. Big time. After tormenting her breasts for a while, he returned to her gasping mouth, inserting his tongue and cupping her cheeks at the same time. It was a long, slow, wet kiss; an intimate and very loving kiss, which Sarah found both incredibly arousing and strangely emotional.

This wasn't just lust, she realised as she clasped Scott close and wallowed in the moment. This was love—honest to goodness, lasting-for-ever love. How could she have ever thought otherwise?

When he finally stopped kissing her, she looked up into his flushed face. 'I do love you, you know,' she said, her stomach going all squishy inside.

'I sure hope so,' he returned, then smiled a wry smile.

'Aren't you going to tell me you love me too?'

'Haven't I already told you that enough already? How many times does a man have to prove himself to you? I love you too.'

Quite a lot, Sarah conceded whilst hugging her happiness, the knowledge that this was love driving her and not just lust bringing a playfulness to their lovemaking that was both fun and exciting.

She could already tell that he liked what she was doing. A lot. Frankly, she'd never seen him so large or so hard.

A choking sound escaped his throat when she bent her head, first to the tip, then to the rest of him, only taking him a few inches before withdrawing then doing it all over again. Gradually, she sucked him in deeper and deeper, but he seemed determined not to surrender, his iron control frustrating her. In the end, Sarah only just managed to take him back into her mouth before he came, shuddering into her as he cried out like a wounded animal, his hands tangling in her hair at the same time.

CHAPTER SIXTEEN

FIFTEEN MINUTES LATER Scott was in pleasurable agony. Perhaps because Sarah had insisted she be on top. The sight of her riding him in a state of such naked abandon did things to him that were almost criminal. Hell, he was going to come if she didn't stop.

His groan carried both agony and ecstasy. 'Hell, Sarah.'

'Sorry. Did I hurt you?'

'You're killing me. Look, just keep still and talk to me for a short while.'

'You don't like to talk, especially during sex.'

'I do right now.'

Sarah sighed an exasperated-sounding sigh. 'But I was having such fun. I've only just learnt how to do this properly and you want me to stop.'

'You'll have lots more opportunity for more practice when you come home with me.'

'*If* I come home with you, don't you mean?' she said archly.

Lord, but she would try the patience of a saint! Maybe he shouldn't bother with her pleasure. Just give in to his own. But damn it all, he didn't have much going for him at the moment except the persuasion of great sex. The trouble was she looked so utterly gorgeous without any clothes on.

Scott loved looking at her. Sarah's body was perfect in every department in Scott's opinion, from her slender shoulders to her tiny waist to the gentle swell of her hips and bottom. And then there were her soft silky thighs and that delicious area in between, which currently had him imprisoned within its hot wet depths.

God. Better not think about that! Otherwise his asking Sarah to stop and talk would not work at all. He was already perilously close to coming.

'Stop wriggling and start talking,' he commanded roughly.

'Truly,' she tut-tutted, lifting her arms to wind her rather dishevelled hair up into a topknot, the action lifting her pretty breasts with their fiercely erect nipples. Her stretching up also lifted her bottom slightly, Scott only just managing not to groan.

'So what do you want me to talk about?' she asked.

'How about telling me how you came to be best friends with Cory?'

'Cory?' she repeated, looking perplexed.

Scott wasn't at all jealous of her close friendship with Cory. He thought it quite sweet. But he *was* curious.

'But I've already told you about Cory. We met at uni and we…well…we had the same interests. Liked the same books and movies.'

Scott could see that she was slightly uncomfortable explaining how their friendship began. 'I get the impression you were more than just friends at one stage,' he said with a burst of intuition.

A guilty colour entered her cheeks.

'Out with it, Sarah,' Scott insisted. 'Honesty, remember?'

'Okay—okay. The truth is I sort of fancied him to begin with. I mean, he was a hunk and by then I think my hormones were willing to bypass my history. So when he asked me out I said yes. Then, when he asked me back to his flat—he wasn't living here yet—I went.'

'Didn't you know he was gay?'

'Not in the slightest. He acted like he found me as attractive as I found him.'

'So what happened when you got back to his flat?'

'Nothing much. We kissed a few times.'

'You *liked* kissing him?'

'I thought I did. I hadn't experienced *your* kisses then, don't forget. I now know that Cory's kisses were like mineral water to your champagne.'

Scott tried not to preen at her compliment. But his male ego was pleased all the same.

'What happened after that?' he asked.

'We moved into his bedroom and started taking off our clothes.'

'And?'

'He broke down and said he was sorry but he couldn't go through with it. He confessed that he was gay but was afraid his parents would hate him and that his life would be ruined. He told me that he'd thought if any girl in the world could make him straight, it would be me. But it hadn't turned out that way. He said he didn't like kissing me and he knew that he wasn't capable of having sex with me.'

'Right. Awkward. What did you do then?'

'I felt like crying but Cory was doing enough for both of us. So I cuddled him and told him he was being silly and that I would go with him to tell his parents the truth the very next day.'

'And did you?'

'Yes, of course. I don't make idle promises. Anyway, they were fine with it. Said they'd already suspected. The upshot was I stayed the day with his family—Cory had two younger sisters—and we all just clicked. We've been good friends ever since.'

'I see,' Scott said. 'So what happened to your hormones after that?' he went on, his curiosity fully whetted by then. 'They sound like they were definitely on the move at last. Not dead and buried any longer.'

'True. But I still wasn't prepared to just jump into bed with anyone. He had to be someone who was physically attractive and whom I could trust with my body. I did look around, believe me, but no one did it for me. Till you came along...'

Scott's heart turned over. Something else stirred as well. Not that his erection had ever really gone to sleep. It had just been distracted for a while. 'I still can't imagine why you found me so attractive. A big, ugly brute like me.'

Sarah's smile was a very Mona Lisa smile. 'You're not at all ugly and you know it. But if you want me to be brutally honest, no pun intended, then I don't know why, either. You were nothing like the fantasy first lover I'd pictured in my head. You were too big and too old and way too intimidating. All I know is that I wanted you from the first moment I set eyes on you.'

'Well, you have me,' he returned thickly. *Till death*

do us part, Scott hoped. 'No more talk now. I have myself under sufficient control to continue, so go ahead and have your wicked way with me…if you so desire.'

'I do so desire, my Lord and master,' she said with a sexy smile, and began riding him again.

Scott clenched his teeth hard in his jaw, determined to outlast her this time.

It was still dark when he woke, his back aching a little from falling asleep on such a hard floor. The rug wasn't thick enough to cushion a man of his size and weight, especially with Sarah sprawled on top of him. The days of his sleeping rough in the outback had long gone. He was used to creature comforts now; used to sleeping in big soft beds in air-conditioned rooms. Sarah too, he imagined. She might have felt wretched during her growing up years but she obviously hadn't wanted for much—materially speaking. Her admitting to having such a substantial amount of money of her own had come as a surprise, but a pleasant one. Clearly, his own financial successes hadn't influenced her feelings for him. She'd said she loved him at first sight and he believed her. A week ago he hadn't been at all sure.

Tonight had certainly shown him how much he loved her. The way he'd felt when she was making love to him had been almost beyond love. Life without her would be impossible. But he felt a little more confident that all would be well. Eventually. Though he suspected Sarah wasn't about to relent about her two weeks' break. Still, he could bear that, now that he had hope.

In the meantime he had to get them both into a proper bed. Not the one downstairs. That was Cory's. Sarah would have been sleeping this past week in the guest room upstairs. Somehow he managed to carry her up the narrow and rather steep staircase without waking her, though she did stir slightly, nuzzling into his neck and muttering something in her dreams. The state of the guest bedroom startled him. First, the bed was covered with clothes. On top of that, the room was on the chilly side. Finally, he succeeded in getting her into the bed, after which he quickly piled the clothes onto a corner chair before diving in after her. She immediately snuggled into him, her body deliciously warm. Scott might have woken her if he hadn't been knackered himself. They'd outdone themselves tonight, making love several times before exhaustion had taken over.

CHAPTER SEVENTEEN

SARAH WAS BROUGHT back slowly to consciousness by Scott shaking her and saying her name.

'Sarah, wake up,' he growled when she kept her eyes dreamily shut, loving the warmth of the thick quilt that enveloped her. 'I need to talk to you, damn you.'

His swearing at her did the trick, her eyes snapping open to see Scott standing beside the bed, glaring down at her. He was naked, except for a towel slung low round his hips, his dripping body and wet hair indicating that he'd just climbed out of a shower. He was also holding the pregnancy testing kit she'd carelessly left on the bathroom vanity.

Oh, dear God…

Sarah swallowed. 'Yes?' she squeaked.

'What's this?' he growled, waggling the box at her.

Sarah's stomach swirled with nausea at the thought he might jump to all the wrong conclusions. Again.

'It's a pregnancy testing kit,' she said, trying her best to sound perfectly innocent and not worried sick.

'No kidding,' came his droll reply. 'I can read, you know. Since we both know it hardly belongs to Cory, then I can only presume you bought it. What I want to know is why? Did you forget to take the pill one night, is that it?' he added, scowling.

'Well, yes and no,' she replied, sitting up slowly whilst holding the bedclothes up over her bare breasts. 'I mean, I didn't just forget one night. I actually haven't taken the pill for some time now.'

His frown darkened. 'And why was that?' he demanded to know.

Sarah knew there was nothing for it but the truth.

'Complacency, security, recklessness. I don't know why. It wasn't until last Saturday that I realised how mistaken I was. But by then taking my pill was the last thing on my mind. I didn't even remember it till you mentioned it last Monday. If you recall, I nearly fainted on the spot. You've no idea how shocked I was at being so stupid. On top of that, I wasn't exactly thrilled at the idea of conceiving a baby through acts of jealousy and revenge. Or even from that lust-crazed quickie we'd just had a few minutes earlier. Though that was preferable, I suppose,' she added bitterly. 'After that, there didn't seem be any point to going back on the pill till my period arrived.'

'Which it obviously hasn't,' Scott said as he shook the box in his hands.

'No,' she agreed wretchedly.

'So, *are* you pregnant?' he asked her. 'Have you taken this test?'

'No. It's too early to tell. I just bought that test on an impulse. The doctor said that I should wait at least another week to be sure.'

'I presume this is the same doctor who prescribed you the antibiotics for your phantom sinus infection,' he said rather caustically.

Guilt had Sarah colouring hotly. 'I had to say something to explain why I couldn't drink at dinner. I knew you knew how much I loved champagne.'

'No kidding. How inventive of you. By then you should have told me the truth, Sarah,' he bit out, his eyes like shiny steel. 'I can almost understand why you didn't tell me straight away after you realised you might have fallen pregnant. You were still mad at me. But I cannot forgive you for keeping it a secret last night. All that talk of honesty and trust over dinner was just so much crap, wasn't it? I'm beginning to think that you were right when you said there was nothing left between us but lust. At least on your part.'

Sarah winced at the coldness in his voice. 'Try to understand my point of view,' she pleaded. 'I didn't tell you about my possibly being pregnant because I didn't want you using it as a weapon to get me to come back before I was ready.'

Sarah knew, the moment the words were out of her mouth, that they were a mistake.

His eyes narrowed even further, his top lip curling up with disgust. 'And wouldn't that have been just criminal!' he threw at her, his voice savage with sarcasm. 'What a terrible thing to do, to ask your wife to come back because she might be having your baby. Totally deplorable! Well, you don't have to worry about that any more, sweetheart. Because I don't think I want you back. Maybe if it turns out you really are pregnant I'll think about it. But just right now I can't even stand to look at you. I'm out of here!' And so saying he threw the testing kit on the bed before storming out of the room.

Stunned by how quickly everything had rocketed

out of control, Sarah stayed where she was, listening to Scott stomping down the stairs, her heart racing, her head spinning with panic-driven thoughts.

I can't let him leave the way I did last Saturday morning. I have to make him see that I do really love him and that I was wrong to lie to him. And that I'm sorry. So terribly, terribly sorry. I should have told him about forgetting the pill and the possibility of a baby straight away.

Silent tears were streaming down her face by the time she bolted out of the bed to run down the stairs after him.

'Go away, Sarah,' he snapped without looking at her, concentrating instead on pulling on his clothes.

'No!' she choked out. 'I will not go away, not till you hear me out.'

Finally, he turned to face her, his shirt in his hands, his cheekbones spotted red with fury. 'There is nothing you have to say that I want to hear.'

'Scott, please…' She glanced down at herself, then lifted her hands to wipe away the tears. 'Sorry.'

The word come out in a ragged sob. Her shoulders started to shake as she peered up at him through flooded eyes. 'Please don't go, Scott. I love you. I've always loved you. I wish I'd told you about the pill business but I was afraid.'

'Of what?'

'Of ending up an emotional mess like my mother. Of never knowing if you really loved me, or you were just staying with me because I was having your baby.'

His face softened then. 'God, Sarah, how could you possibly think that? A baby would be nice, but it wouldn't make me love you more. Or want you more. It's you I married, Sarah. *You.*'

He dropped the shirt and gathered her tenderly into his arms, warming her trembling body with his own.

'I think it's time I took you home,' he murmured as he stroked her hair down her back. 'What do you say, Sarah?'

'Yes, please,' she blubbered against his bare chest.

'Everything will be all right now,' he said as he stroked her. 'Trust me.'

CHAPTER EIGHTEEN

SCOTT WAS GLAD they had two cars to accommodate all of Sarah's things. Lord, but he had no idea how she'd crammed everything into that small car of hers, despite it being a hatchback. It was full to the brim yet his car still had clothes draped all over his back seat and boxes of shoes piled high on the passenger seat. Thank goodness he'd been able to find a parking spot close to Cory's house last night, otherwise packing would have been a slow process.

'Ready to go now?' he asked Sarah as she stood next to her car, frowning as though she'd forgotten something.

'Just have to get one last thing,' she said without looking at him.

'Okay. I'll wait here for you.'

Her reappearance with the dreaded pregnancy kit in her hands reminded Scott how close he'd come to wrecking any chance of a reconciliation after he'd found that damned thing in the bathroom. Just the sight of it still raised his blood pressure a notch, but he clenched his mouth tightly shut, making no comment as she put it in her own car. But it took a real effort to control himself. By the time they climbed in behind their respective wheels and drove off, Scott was relieved to be in a separate car to Sarah for the drive home. That way he wouldn't say anything inflammatory to her the way he had earlier.

It also gave him the opportunity to think about things.

It wasn't like him to lose his temper like that. He was usually way more pragmatic, priding himself on his ability to stay calm under pressure. His father had been a laid-back fellow, rarely raising his voice and never being violent in any way, except when pushed to the limit. Though he confessed he *had* hit the roof when he'd discovered the existence of a secret son—a very neglected secret son. Still, that was understandable. No one liked seeing children—especially their own—being mistreated.

Scott had always believed he was a chip off the old block. Ugly outbursts of anger were simply not his style, though, damn it all, he'd been sorely tested ever since those wretched photos had arrived. He'd certainly been tested that day in Leighton's office. And tested too by Sarah's own highly emotional and sometimes contrary behaviour. He'd really seen red this morning once he'd realised she'd lied to him the previous night over dinner, especially when she'd gone on and on about trust and honesty.

Still, in hindsight, he could see why she hadn't told him about her possible pregnancy. And, yes, he could understand that during the distress of last weekend's events all thought of the pill and falling pregnant had gone right out of her head. But once she'd remembered she should have told him. No question about that. And she shouldn't have made up all that rubbish about having a sinus infection and not being able to drink because she was on antibiotics.

A wry laugh escaped his lips at the sheer inventiveness of her lie. She'd make a fabulous trial lawyer one day, no doubt about that. And a good mother too, no doubt, if and when the time came. Sarah would want to do everything right. Scott figured he'd make a pretty good father, too. He'd had a very good example. Frankly, now that he thought about it more calmly, Scott wasn't unhappy about Sarah having forgotten her pill. A baby would be good for them both. They'd always planned to have a baby. One day. When Sarah's career was more established and when she was ready for it.

Maybe that was the reason behind Sarah's panic. Because she wasn't ready for parenthood. Or more likely, she believed *he* wasn't. An understandable belief, given he'd been spending so much time away on business. Scott could see now that he'd been neglecting her. Neglecting her *and* his marriage. He'd started taking her for granted. No wonder she'd thought he was having an affair. And no wonder he'd believed *she* was. He could see now why she'd bolted, why she was worried about their future relationship.

Scott sighed. Maybe he should tell her that. Admit his failings and at least talk to her a lot more, reassuring her that things would change in future. And he would keep telling her he wouldn't mind a bit if she was already pregnant, as long as she didn't. The only difficulty was how to bring such a topic up in the conversation without it seeming forced, or false.

Scott felt lucky when an opportunity for such a conversation came up as he was helping Sarah unpack her car. Perversely, it was the pregnancy testing kit—which Sarah had thrown onto the floor in front of the passenger seat—which did the trick. Picking it up, he started to read the instructions on the back of the box.

'It says here,' he remarked, doing his best to sound casual, 'that this is a very sensitive test and can pick up a pregnancy quite early.'

Sarah sighed as she took the box out of his hands. 'Yes, I've already read all that. The girl in the chemist shop said it was the best. But the doctor said it can still give a false negative if you take the test before your next period is due.'

'But it might not,' he countered. 'And let's face it, you don't know when your next period is due. You've totally stuffed up your hormones. Maybe you should just take the test and see.'

Anxiety was instantly etched on Sarah's lovely face. 'I don't want to do that, Scott. I keep thinking about the horrible argument we had last week. What if I fell pregnant that Friday night? What if this baby was conceived in anger and revenge? I wouldn't like that so I'd rather not know yet, thank you very much.'

'I can understand your feelings on that subject, Sarah,' Scott said in reassuring tones, 'but maybe it's time for you to rethink what happened that night. Look, we'd both had scares that day over our love for each other and we both wanted to lay claim to each other the way men and women have been doing since time began. With sex. If you recall, you were as provocative as I was demanding.'

Sarah frowned, her expression thoughtful, his carefully reasoned words obviously striking a chord with her intelligent brain.

'Well, yes,' she said slowly. 'Yes, I do see that that's what *I* was doing, anyway. I was seriously rocked by the thought that you were having an affair with Cleo.'

'How do you think I felt when I looked at those photos?' he pointed out, deliberately keeping his voice calm.

She pulled a face. 'Mmm. Yes. They were pretty damning. Cory told me you were just acting like any man would have, but I wouldn't listen to him.'

'You should have, Sarah. Cory's a smart man. But back to our rethinking the events that Friday night. You can't deny that it was great sex. The best we'd had so far. Though last night was pretty darned good too.'

Scott loved it when she blushed. His virgin bride was still deliciously enchanting.

'Trust me,' he went on, 'when I say that along with my feelings of jealousy and anger that night, I never stopped loving you. Never! If we made a baby that night then it will definitely be a baby born of love.'

'Oh,' she said, and promptly burst into tears. Which was not quite the reaction Scott had in mind.

Suppressing a groan, he gathered her into his arms and held her close. She wept for a while but not for too long, gathering herself reasonably quickly, he thought, then reaching up to kiss him on the cheek.

Such a simple kiss but it moved him, touching his soul more than any of the passionate kisses she'd given him last night. Because it was full of forgiveness. And love. A pure, sweet, loving love. Nothing to do with lust.

'Thank you for that,' she said as she smiled softly up at him. 'And I love you too. Very much. And I'm not so worried any more about being pregnant. What you said just now… It…it made all the difference.'

'I hope so, Sarah,' he returned, not entirely convinced that she felt truly happy about falling pregnant that night. Which was fair enough. It hadn't exactly been a night of romance. His lovemaking had been raw and, yes, vengeful. There was no denying it. But the passion and love behind his jealousy had been real. God, yes. 'I still feel I haven't said enough how sorry I am for not trusting you.'

'Stop now,' she replied quickly, and laid a gentle hand on the cheek she'd just kissed. 'They say love is never having to say you're sorry.'

He laughed. 'Now that's a load of old rubbish. I should have crawled on my hands and knees to beg your forgiveness. I know I crossed the line that night and my feeble attempt to whitewash my behaviour is totally unacceptable.'

'True. But we have to move past all that now, Scott. I'm ready to. Honest.'

'Honest?' he echoed, and smiled a wry smile.

'Absolutely,' she said. 'Aside from your heartfelt apology just now, I had some time to get my head together on the drive over here. I feel much better about our marriage and I've come to a decision.'

Scott swallowed. 'And what decision is that?'

'As soon as we get the last of these things upstairs, I'm going to go take that test.'

CHAPTER NINETEEN

SARAH REGRETTED HER decision the moment she made it. But it was too late to back out now. With fumbling fingers she opened the box and extracted the white plastic stick. For a long moment she just stared at it, as if it was a fearful thing. Which it was. A powerful, fearful thing that had the power to make her feel… *what*, exactly? Happy? Unhappy? Confused? Impatient? Or all of those things. Did she want the test to be negative, or positive? She wasn't sure any more. Wasn't sure of anything except that Scott loved her.

So she clung to that reassurance and rather numbly did what the instructions said to do. But as she waited for the hormones to give her a result a truly weird sensation came over Sarah; a light-headedness that left her dizzy and dazed and just a little disoriented. She had to sit down on the toilet again—quickly— leaning forward till enough time had passed for her to reach for the stick.

Her face drained of more blood as she stared at it.

Scott could not believe how tense he was, waiting for Sarah to come out of the bathroom. He paced the bedroom like an expectant father in a maternity ward. When she finally emerged, her face was pale but she wasn't crying or anything. She just looked… shocked.

'Well?' he prompted when she didn't say anything.

'Yes,' she choked out, nodding rather blankly. 'It was pink. Very pink.'

'Wow!' Scott exclaimed, beaming over at her. 'Wow!'

'I'm going to have a baby,' she said in stunned tones. 'A real baby.'

'So it seems, sweetheart,' he said, then strode over and scooped her up in his arms, whirling her round and laughing as he hadn't done in ages. It took him a little while to realise Sarah wasn't laughing.

He planted her back down on her feet and looked at her with suddenly worried eyes. 'You are happy about the baby, aren't you?' he asked anxiously. 'You're not still upset over…you know…' His voice trailed off, his heart squeezing tight at the thought she might still hate the idea of having conceived a baby that Friday night.

She blinked up at him a couple of times, then slowly, wonderfully, she smiled. 'No, I'm not upset about that any more. I wasn't lying when I said your lovely words made all the difference. It's just that I didn't think I would feel quite this…overwhelmed. It's one thing to imagine you might be pregnant, but when you know you definitely are, it's an entirely different feeling. Most girls fantasise about becoming mothers but the reality of it is a little daunting. I…I hope I'll make a good mother.'

'You'll make a terrific one.'

'I would like to think so. Still…it's a big thing, having a baby, isn't it? It changes your life.'

'Only for the better,' he reassured her gently. 'We'll become a family, Sarah. Our own family, to fashion the way we want it to be. Neither of us have families. Now it's you and me and little whatsit.'

'Whatsit?' Sarah threw him a pretend scowl. 'Our baby is not a *whatsit*. It's a boy or girl. Or both.'

'It can't be both,' Scott snorted.

'Unless it's twins,' she exclaimed in a startled tone.

'Good Lord! But that would be awesome. Or maybe you're just a very fertile little minx. Either way it's still good news, isn't it?'

'What? Oh, yes…yes. I suppose so.'

'You seem a bit stunned by the idea.'

'I am. I really am.' Her hand lifted to wipe her pale forehead. 'I've gone a bit dizzy, all of a sudden.'

'Could be because you haven't had any breakfast. And neither have I. I'll get you a glass of juice. Then let's drop everything and walk up to Dino's and have a celebratory eat-up.' Dino's was a trendy little café not far from their building, which served breakfast all day every day as well as the most delicious pancakes. They often had breakfast there on the weekends. Lunch too. With the sun out and the day promising some pre-winter warmth they could sit at one of the outdoor tables in the back courtyard. They weren't that popular because of the noise that came from nearby Luna Park, but neither of them minded the sounds of happiness.

'I'd like that,' Sarah said, then shook her head. 'Twins!' she exclaimed as he took her elbow and steered her out into the kitchen.

'Could be,' he told her. 'My father was a twin.'

'You never told me that.'

'Didn't I?'

'No.'

He shrugged. 'I'll tell you over brunch.'

CHAPTER TWENTY

'WELL?' SARAH PROMPTED as soon as they'd ordered their food and sat down at one of their favourite outdoor tables.

'Well, what?' he replied.

'You were going to tell me about your father being a twin.'

'Oh, yes, so I was,' he said with a cheeky smile. 'They weren't identical twins. Similar in looks, but nothing like each other in nature, Dad said. His name was Roger and he was a right rebel. A risk taker. He died when he was eighteen. Got killed falling off a motorcycle.'

'That's sad. But I don't know about their being all that different in nature. Your dad didn't exactly follow the conventional path in life, did he?'

'Well, no, but he wasn't a risk taker.'

'Really? Then why did he buy old mines and plots of land which everyone said were useless?'

He frowned at her, then laughed. 'I never told you that, madam, so where did you get that little nugget of information from?'

Sarah grinned. 'Remember the day we met?'

'I'm hardly likely to forget it,' he said in droll

tones. 'It was very difficult to sit in that boardroom, conducting business with a hard-on the size of Centrepoint Tower.'

'Hush up,' a blushing Sarah said as she looked hurriedly over at the nearest table, which was occupied by a couple and their two small children. 'There are children here.'

'Sorry. Okay, out with it.'

'Well, I was bored to tears that day and had nothing better to do than look you up on the Internet. Not that it was all that informative. You really are not very communicative with the media, are you? I couldn't even find a decent photo—just one with a hard hat on where you looked like a union leader. A rather weather-beaten one. Trust me when I tell you I wasn't impressed. I didn't fancy you at all till I saw you in the flesh. Not sure why I did then, either. You were a long way from being my fantasy man.'

'That's sweet of you to say so.'

'I did tell you that I was going to be honest from now on.'

Scott laughed. 'In a selective manner, that is.'

'I promise I will tell only little white lies in future.'

'That's a comfort. So what did you fancy about me, once you saw me in the flesh?'

'Just about everything, I guess. But most of all I liked the way you looked at me. It made me feel very…sexy.'

'Yet you held out on me till our third date.'

'I didn't want you to think I was easy.'

'Sweetheart, have you forgotten you were a virgin?'

'No. But you didn't know that at the time.'

'You'd be right there. I was quite blown away once I found out.'

'You *were* rather surprised.'

'True. I'd never come across one before.'

'Not even when you were younger?'

'Nah. I was into older women at that stage.'

'And now?'

'Now I'm just into you.' His smile was wonderful and warm, with just a hint of wicked promise. Sarah suspected that as soon as they got back home she wouldn't be putting all her things away till much later. Scott would be whisking her off to bed. She recognised that glint in his eye only too well.

Their food arrived, hers a simple serving of poached eggs and fried mushrooms on toast whilst Scott was presented with a huge pile of pancakes with a side dish of vanilla ice cream. Sarah knew that all conversation would cease till Scott had eaten. Already his whole concentration was on pouring the maple syrup onto the first pancake, his steely grey eyes lighting up as his taste buds salivated.

Sarah didn't mind his obsessed state, using the quiet to enjoy her own food, taking her time and washing each delicious mouthful down with some freshly squeezed orange juice. Scott was still eating when she finished, so Sarah put down her cutlery, leant back in her seat and admired her surroundings. It was lovely and warm where they were sitting, the sounds of laughter and rides from Luna Park adding to her happiness.

And she *was* happy. Happier than she'd been in her whole life. If anyone had told her she would have felt this happy a little over a week ago, she would not have believed them.

And it wasn't just because of the baby. Or babies, if it turned out she was having twins. Her happiness came from the new depth of understanding that she'd forged with Scott. She felt confident now that their marriage would go the distance. And that was very important to her, especially now that she was having a baby. She personally didn't want to ever suffer the wretchedness of divorce. She certainly didn't want her children to have to endure the distress and lone-liness of their parents' separating.

There was only one thing that still bothered her a bit, but which she didn't want to address at this stage. Why risk spoiling things today? But sooner or later she would have to tell Scott that she wanted the fa-ther of her children to be a more stay-at-home dad, not going away on business trips all the time with his PA. Weirdly, as though reading her mind, Scott him-self brought the subject up over coffee.

'I've been thinking,' he said, 'that in future, I'm going to cut down on going away on business.'

'I'd really like that,' Sarah said. 'It did annoy me how often you were going away. And how you always took Cleo and never asked me,' she added, trying not to sound jealous, but not entirely succeeding.

Scott frowned at her. 'I didn't think you'd be able to drop everything at your work and come with me.'

'I suppose I can't. Not always. But I would have liked you to ask occasionally.'

'Point taken. Look, I'm in the process of finding myself a business partner. I *was* looking for more of a silent money-bags-type partner but instead I'll

look for someone who wants to be more hands-on.
That way he can take some of the load off me when
it comes to going away. How does that sound?'

'It sounds good,' she said.

'We'll also have to buy a proper family home.
Can't raise a family in an apartment. We'll need a
yard. One big enough for a dog. Got to have a dog.
I always had a dog when I was growing up. A kid
needs a dog.'

'I always wanted a dog, but Mum refused to get
one. Said they dropped hair all over the place.'

'We'll find one that doesn't drop hair.'

'Gosh, this is all so exciting. Can we go look at
some family homes this afternoon?'

'Nope. Once you finish your coffee we're going
home. And then we're going to bed.'

CHAPTER TWENTY-ONE

'WHERE ARE YOU GOING?' Scott asked when Sarah suddenly threw back the bedclothes and climbed out of bed.

They'd made love on and off all afternoon, Scott being extra gentle, Sarah laughing at his worry over *disturbing the babes*. Nothing too athletic or too deep was the order of the day.

'But they wouldn't be the size of two peas yet,' she told him at one stage when she'd wanted to be on top. 'And there might only be one pea.'

Scott didn't say anything at the time but he felt absolutely certain that she'd conceived twins, the same way he'd been certain that that diamond mine he'd bought a year ago would prove not to be the worked-out dud everyone else imagined. And he'd been right. Already it was showing a decent profit. Scott believed he was right about Sarah having twins as well. Which thrilled him no end.

Strange, really. Having children had never been a huge urge for Scott. Neither had marriage, for that matter. But everything had changed once he met Sarah.

An image formed in his mind of how it would

be, standing by Sarah's side as she pushed two tiny babies into the world. His heart swelled with love at the thought. Love and pride.

It amazed him how excited he felt about becoming a father, now that it was actually happening to him for real. Scott aimed to give his own children the same things his father had given him. Plenty of time spent with them, a degree of discipline, lots of love and, yes, definitely a dog.

Not that he planned on spoiling his children. That didn't work. He'd seen the results of rich parents spoiling their children and it wasn't pretty.

So no spoiling, except in matters of time and love. Sarah was right about his cutting down on those business trips, though. Hopefully, Cleo would be able to find him that hands-on business partner before long.

The bathroom door opened and Sarah emerged, quickly diving back under the covers where she cuddled up to him. This time they just talked, trying to work out what suburbs they would buy a house in.

'I do like the northern beaches,' he said, 'but the traffic is always awful. It would take us for ever to get to work.'

'True. But it is nice on the north side, especially the beachside suburbs. Why don't we look for a suburb which has a good ferry service?' Sarah suggested. 'Manly Beach maybe. Then we wouldn't even have to drive to work. We could catch the ferry together and hold hands.'

Bringing up the subject of work put a slight dent in Scott's contentment. The thought of Sarah continuing to work in the same firm as that snake Leighton did not sit well with him. But he just knew she wouldn't like his asking her to quit again. So he didn't. Not right at that moment. But he suspected it wouldn't be long before he said something. He wasn't the kind of man who would let his wife continue being in the company of a man like that.

'I suppose we should get up,' Sarah said with a resigned sigh. 'I need to hang up my clothes properly. We just dumped them on the floor of the walk-in wardrobe, remember?'

Scott remembered. 'I'll help you,' he said, 'then we should eat again. I don't know about you but I'm starving.'

'You're always starving,' she said smilingly. 'But you're right. I am a bit hungry.'

'That's because you're eating for three.'

Sarah punched him in the ribs. 'Will you stop saying that? We don't know it's twins.'

'No. We don't. It might be triplets.'

He laughed at the look of horror that crossed her face.

'Don't even *think* such a thing,' she chastised. 'Now, no more of that nonsense. Time to get up and get to work.'

Scott winced. That *work* word again. Hell on earth, but just the thought of Sarah being anywhere near that bastard brought out his caveman side. Still, it wasn't the right moment to bring the subject up. She seemed so happy.

He should have known that he wouldn't be able to keep his big mouth shut for long.

CHAPTER TWENTY-TWO

'HOW ON EARTH did you get all this stuff in your one little car?' Scott asked her as he helped her put away her clothes properly.

'Fury, I suppose,' Sarah said with a shrug. 'I just jammed it all in.'

'You really were very angry with me.'

Sarah's mind flew back to that Saturday morning when he'd shown her those photos. It seemed a life-time ago now. 'You have no idea,' she confessed. 'I could cheerfully have killed you.'

'I deserved killing.'

'Indeed. But perhaps I should have stayed and had it out with you instead of flouncing off the way I did.' Sarah was finally forced to face that she'd al-ways run away from distressing situations rather than confronting them. Hopefully, she wasn't going to be like that any more.

'I think the blame rests wholly and solely on me, my darling,' he said. 'I was totally in the wrong.'

'But with mitigating circumstances,' she said.

Scott smiled. 'Spoken like a lawyer. By the way, did you let Cory know the good news?'

'No,' she said, clearly astonished with herself. 'I forgot.'

'Better let him know, don't you think?'

'He can wait till later this evening. It's only just after five. He's probably still in the conference, learning how to build some more icons like the Opera House.'

'True. Okay, I'll go see what I can rustle up for an early dinner whilst you finish up here,' he suggested.

'Sounds like a good plan.'

Sarah was humming happily as she put her shoes away in her walk-in wardrobe when she suddenly came across the anniversary present that she'd bought Scott and never given him. She'd originally hidden it at the back of one of the shelves, planning to give it to him on the morning of their anniversary. Now, she picked up the small plastic bag in which lay the even smaller box, her heart filling as she went in search of Scott. She found him perched up on a kitchen stool, searching his phone for something.

'All finished?' he asked without glancing up.

'Just about,' she replied, clutching the plastic bag with suddenly nervous hands. What if he didn't like what she'd bought?

'So what would you like me to order in to eat?' he asked her, finally looking up. 'There's nothing much in the fridge or the cupboards to cook with. I've been living the life of a lazy bachelor whilst you were away, not going to the supermarket and existing on take-away. Thank God for the cleaning service, that's all I can say, or you'd be coming home to a tip. I was lost without you, my darling. Totally, utterly lost. So what's it to be? Thai, Chinese, Indian?'

Sarah's stomach turned over at the thought of anything spicy. 'Could we just have toast and pumpkin soup?' she requested. 'I know that's there. And you can follow up with some of your favourite chocolate ice cream. We always have heaps of that in the freezer.'

'Done!' he said, smiling. 'So what's that you have there?'

'It…it's the anniversary present I bought you. It's not wrapped up, I'm afraid,' she added, and walked over to sit down on the stool next to him.

She handed him the plastic bag and watched, her heart thudding, as he drew out the small black leather box. His eyebrows arched. 'Jewellery, Sarah?'

Sarah knew Scott wasn't a ring-wearer. Had refused to have a wedding ring. But the moment she'd seen this particular ring in the shop window, she'd felt compelled to buy it. Perhaps because it represented the stability and security she'd always experienced with Scott but which had been seriously rocked that day.

'Yes,' she said, her voice firmer than her emotions. 'I hope you like it.'

Scott determined to like it, no matter what it was. But when he flipped open the lid of the box and saw what lay inside, *liking* was not even close to his emotion.

It was a man's ring. A gold ring, with an intricately woven design on top that looked like an eight on its side. Scott knew what the sign meant. It was the mathematical symbol of infinity. His father had taught him maths as a kid, drawing all the symbols and signs in the sandy outback soil with a stick. This one had intrigued Scott at the time, his father explaining that the continuous loop meant it never ended.

'But that doesn't make sense, Dad,' he'd said. 'Nothing goes on and on for ever.'

'Numbers do,' came his father's logical reply. 'And space.'

And true love, Scott thought, a lump in his throat.

'I love it,' he said as he slipped it on the bare third finger of his left hand, surprised that it fitted. Smiling, he leant over to kiss her on the cheek. 'It's perfect. Like you.'

'I'm not at all perfect,' Sarah replied, smiling back at him. 'But I do love you. I will love you till the end of time. That's what this ring represents to me. Our everlasting love.'

When Scott's face fell Sarah almost panicked. Had she been over the top with her declaration? Didn't he love her the way she loved him?

'God, Sarah,' he said, turning the ring round and round on his finger. 'Now I feel awful. I didn't buy you anything at all. I forgot. I'm so sorry.'

'It doesn't matter,' she said. 'Presents don't matter. Not really.'

'I think they do. Getting this lovely present showed me that. I'll buy you something tomorrow, my darling. Something special. And we'll go somewhere extra special tomorrow night for dinner.'

'It'll be Monday night,' she pointed out. 'Most of the good restaurants are closed on a Monday night.'

'Yes, you're right,' he mused. 'Tomorrow's Monday…'

His eyes carried worry as he looked deep into hers.

'You won't reconsider not working for that mob any more? I can't stand the thought of you being anywhere near that Leighton bastard.'

Sarah stiffened. She understood completely that Scott didn't want her working in the same building as Phil. And to tell the truth, she had her doubts about staying at Goldstein & Evans as well, now that she was pregnant. They were a rather gung-ho legal firm who expected their employees to give one hundred and ten per cent. And whilst Sarah was a dedicated lawyer who enjoyed her work, her priorities had changed with her pregnancy. But it was a matter of principle that she go to work the following morning. A matter of her husband trusting her, not of her just doing what he ordered her to do like some old-fashioned chauvinist.

'I'm sorry, Scott,' she told him soothingly. 'I understand your feelings entirely. But I will be going to work tomorrow morning. I can't just up and quit. It would make it very hard for me to get another job. People would think I was flighty and unreliable. But you're right. I will start looking around for another position, okay?'

'Okay,' he said with decided reluctance in his voice.

'Trust me,' she said.

'I do trust you,' he countered. 'I just don't trust Leighton.'

CHAPTER TWENTY-THREE

DESPITE SARAH ARRIVING at work a good fifteen minutes before the official start time of eight-thirty the next morning, the place was already abuzz, with most of the offices filled with busy, busy people. For the first time since her early days of working at Goldstein & Evans, Sarah experienced a totally negative reaction towards the atmosphere. She didn't find it heady the way she once had. Just hectic.

Several people asked her how she was feeling after her week off, but none of the queries seemed sincere, no one actually stopping to speak to her for more than a few seconds as she walked past. It also bothered her that she couldn't just dump her handbag and head off to the staff room to use the coffee machine the way she usually did. Fear of running into Phil there had forced her to buy herself a takeaway coffee downstairs instead.

Sarah slumped down at her desk, annoyed with that fear, annoyed with herself for not realising sooner that Phil did fancy her. If she had, she wouldn't have used his shoulder to cry on whenever Scott went away on business. But she had. Stupidly. She hadn't encouraged his interest, but she hadn't discouraged him, either.

Not that that gave him any excuse to do what he'd done. Had he honestly thought she'd run to him, if and when her marriage broke up? She'd never fancied him. Never! Now she actively hated him, the way she hated her slime bag father and brother. Sarah regretted that she'd never confronted either of them and told them what she thought of them. Instead, they'd got away with the reprehensible way they'd both behaved. She should have at least torn verbal strips off them. Not that it would have dented their consciences one iota. It would have been water off a duck's back. But at least it would have given her some satisfaction. And made her feel slightly better.

Phil shouldn't get away with what he'd done, either.

Gripping her large takeaway coffee with both hands, Sarah stood up and walked slowly out into the main corridor, turning right and heading towards the family law section, sipping as she went. Adrenaline had her heart racing, all her inner muscles tightening as she drew closer to Phil's office.

His very attractive secretary was at her desk, looking rather smug as usual.

'Is Phil in, Janice?' Sarah asked politely enough.

'He's busy,' she replied sharply as she looked Sarah up and down.

'I need to speak to him,' Sarah went on. 'Could you please let him know that I'm here?'

Just then the door to Phil's office opened and the man himself walked out, his eyes also running over Sarah, though not with the same hostile regard as his secretary. 'I thought I heard your voice,' he said with an oily smile. 'Did you want to see me?'

Sarah had no intention of confronting him in front

of Janice, so she smiled back at him, hiding the way her skin crawled at his almost lascivious appraisal. Sarah knew she looked good. She always looked good when she came to work. Today's outfit was a pale pink Chanel suit, matched with a cream silk blouse that had a ruffle framing the pearl-buttoned front, a style that flattered her willowy figure and her fair colouring. Her hair was up in a neat roll and her make-up was perfect, her perfume subtle yet sexy. Elegant pearl drops fell from her neat lobes.

Sarah didn't object to men giving her admiring looks but she hated being ogled. Her stomach tightened with rage, but still she smiled.

'Yes, I do want to see you, Phil,' she said sweetly. 'I'm in need of some legal advice.'

His eyes lit up with pleasure, not compassion. 'Of course, dear girl. Anything for you. Do come in.' He waved her into his office. 'Hold all calls, will you, Janice?'

The back of Sarah's neck prickled as she walked into the office and Phil closed the door behind her.

'Why don't we sit over here?' he said, directing her to a long grey leather sofa that rested against a far wall. His office was one of the largest, his status very high in the firm.

She didn't object, despite her skin crawling some more. He sat unnecessarily close to her, his expression full of feigned concern. He might have picked up one of her hands if they hadn't both been cupped tightly around her coffee.

'You don't have to tell me what the problem is,' he started straight away. 'You've left your husband, haven't you?'

'I…yes…I did.' Not a lie. She had. For a while.

'I'm not surprised. You may or may not know this but your husband came to see me last week and made all sorts of vile accusations about some photos someone sent him. Photos of you and me at the Regency hotel that Friday lunchtime.'

'He did tell me about his visit to you,' Sarah admitted stiffly.

'Did he tell you that he threatened to kill me if I came near you ever again?'

'No, he didn't,' Sarah confessed, slightly shocked at Scott's threat.

'You're well out of that marriage, Sarah. Look, I know that you didn't come to work all last week and it worried the life out of me, thinking what that bully of a husband might have done to you. The thought of his abusing you in some way gave me nightmares.'

'Scott would *never* hit me,' she defended hotly, thinking that if Phil was so worried about her then why hadn't he tried to call her?

She understood full well why he hadn't. First, he didn't really care about her. And second, Scott had scared the living daylights out of him.

'I wouldn't be too sure of that,' he sneered. 'McAllister comes from a rough and tough background. He has violence written all over him. You could do so much better, my dear,' he said, then actually dared to place his hand on her knee. 'You deserve a man who would appreciate you as his wife, someone who would give you the kind of life to complement your beauty and your brains.'

'And are you imagining that that man would be you, Phil?' she asked him, struggling to keep the dislike out of her voice. She hadn't set out to trap him into incriminating himself, but couldn't resist the temptation.

That disgusting hand on her knee actually moved in what he no doubt thought was a seductive circle.

'You must know how I feel about you, Sarah,' he murmured, his eyes locking with hers. 'I've admired you ever since you came to work here. You are the kind of woman any man would want. When you married McAllister I couldn't believe it. The man has no class, or culture. He's nothing but a thug in a suit. But at least now you've seen the error of your ways and you've finally come to me. *Finally*,' he repeated, that horrible hand daring to inch up onto her thigh.

Sarah could not bear another second of his vile touch, slapping his hand away and jumping to her feet at the same time. 'My God, you don't honestly think I would leave Scott for you, do you?' she threw at him, only just stopping herself from throwing the coffee at him as well. 'Even if your rotten plan had worked and Scott and I broke up permanently, I would never turn to you.'

He seemed totally thrown by her outburst, his massive ego clearly unable to take in exactly what she was saying.

'But you said you left him,' he blurted out. 'You came to me and said you wanted a divorce.'

'I did leave Scott,' she countered furiously. 'But we're back together again now, stronger than ever. Your appalling plan didn't work in the end. And I *never* asked for a divorce. I said I wanted some legal advice. So tell me, Phil, what would you advise a girl in my position to do? You do realise that Mr Goldstein is not too partial to claims of sexual harassment against his employees.'

Sarah saw the instant fear in his eyes and knew Scott had his character pegged right. The man was a total sleaze and an out-and-out coward.

'You have no proof of anything,' he said shakily as he stood up. 'It's your word against mine.'

'Is it just? Well, maybe my word might have more sway with the boss than yours.'

'If you go to Goldstein, you'll be making a big mistake,' he spat at her. 'My father is an important man, a senator and a very close friend of his. You won't win.'

'Oh, lovely. And there I was, thinking you must be mad about me to do what you did.'

'I'm not that mad about any woman,' he snarled, his handsome face twisted into an ugly mask. 'Lord knows what I was thinking,' he went on nastily, shrugging his shoulders and straightening his tie as he looked down his finely chiselled nose at her. 'You might be beautiful, sweetheart, but you obviously don't have any taste. Fancy taking up with that big lug when you could have had me. The mind boggles.'

Her mind certainly did. God, the arrogance of the man! And the sheer vanity.

'Scott is more of a man than you'll ever be,' she stated firmly. 'What's laughable is that I used to like you. I thought you were my friend, someone I could turn to for advice. I couldn't believe it at first when Scott said you'd set me up so that I would look like a cheater. But I soon saw that he was right. Though he was wrong about your motive. You never really wanted me, did you? You just wanted to cause trouble.

To make me miserable. It was all because I'd bruised your male ego.'

His laugh was scoffing. 'Well, it certainly wasn't because I couldn't live without you. But I was sick to death of your complaining about hubby going away all the time, so I decided to give you something to really complain about. Which reminds me. Your husband could be having an affair with his PA, for all I know. I didn't have him investigated at all. That was just an excuse to get you to go to the hotel with me. My main aim was for your stupid husband to think *you* were having an affair. I figured if in the fallout I managed to get a bit of that delicious arse of yours then I'd count that as a bonus.'

Sarah managed somehow not to reel back. 'Scott was right,' she said coldly. 'You are disgusting.'

Fear zoomed back into his eyes. 'You can't prove anything.'

'Maybe not, but mud sticks, Phil.'

'It sure does. What if I say you did sleep with me that day? That you told me you loved me and you were going to leave your husband for me, but I told you I didn't love you back—that everything you're now saying is just the revenge of a woman scorned.'

Sarah shook her head. Scott had been so right. Leighton was a slimy bastard who wasn't to be trusted. For a moment she felt rattled, but then she reminded herself that she'd faced slimier men in court.

'I'd say you'd be wasting your breath,' she returned coolly. 'Because I'm out of here as of now. You're not worth the hassle of a law suit. Or anything else. Time will take care of you. I just wanted the opportunity to see you face-to-face and tell you what I think of you before I resigned.'

'You're resigning?' he asked, his mouth dropping open.

'I sure am. And I won't be back.'

'But what reason will you give for resigning?'

Her smile was a little wicked. Let the creep worry.

'Oh, I'll think of something,' she said airily, and with that she whirled and marched over to the door, flinging it open to find Janice standing right next to the door, obviously listening to what had gone on. The girl's face was flushed and she seemed quite upset. Sarah, however, had never felt better. There was something very cathartic about having some revenge, no matter how small, on the man who'd almost ruined her marriage.

'I'd stop sleeping with him if I were you,' Sarah called over her shoulder as she strode off, tossing the half-drunk coffee in a nearby bin on the way. 'The man's a total sleazebag and a big-time loser.'

CHAPTER TWENTY-FOUR

SARAH'S SMILE WAS wide as she walked the three blocks to Scott's office. God, but it felt so good to be out of there, and not just because she'd escaped Phil's toxic presence. Sarah hadn't appreciated till this moment that she hadn't been overly enjoying her job for some time. She'd liked some of her clients and cases, but not the constant pressure of having to win. Goldstein & Evans had a 'win at all costs' policy, which could be wearing after a while. They also expected you to work long hours, without getting paid overtime. Which had been fine by her to begin with. But it wasn't the sort of workplace she envisaged enduring once she had a baby.

Whilst Sarah didn't want to abandon her career entirely for motherhood, neither did she want to be one of those mothers who gave over all the caring of her children to nannies and day-care centres. That wasn't the kind of family life she craved. If she expected Scott to stay home more, then the same should apply to her. Sarah believed in equality in a marriage.

Sarah didn't ring Scott to tell him she was coming, keeping the news of her resignation as a surprise. He was going to be so pleased, she thought as she rode the lift up to his floor. Her smile was still in place as she pushed open the door that had McAllister Mines written on it in silver lettering.

'Hi, Leanne,' she said happily to the forty-something receptionist. 'The boss in?'

'Sure is.'

'Great. Looking good, Leanne. New hairdresser?' Leanne was sporting a chin-length honey-brown bob with blonde highlights, which was more youthful than her previous style.

'Yes. *Yours*. Thanks for the tip.'

'My pleasure.'

Sarah made her way down the corridor to Cleo's door. When knocking elicited no answer, she popped her head inside, only to find the office empty. The door into Scott's office was open, however, and what Sarah saw in there had the ready smile fading from her face. For there was Cleo, standing in front of Scott's desk, wrapped in Scott's arms. One of his hands rested in the small of her back, the other was stroking her thick dark hair with what looked like tenderness. He was murmuring something soft and reassuring, and Cleo... Cleo sounded as if she was crying.

Instantly, the most horrible thoughts rushed through Sarah's head.

They are *having an affair.*

It's been going on for ages.

Scott has just told her about the baby and Cleo is devastated.

Sarah's first reaction was to turn and run. Maybe she could hide in the powder room for a while and come back later. Pretend she hadn't seen a thing.

A few days ago, she might have. But not today.

Today was the beginning of the first day of her new marriage, one which embraced honesty and total trust, not with wild bursts of jealousy.

Taking a deep gathering breath, Sarah calmed her mind, letting common sense push aside those other hasty and quite irrational thoughts.

Of course they are not having an affair.

Scott loves you and Cleo isn't that kind of woman.

You have to trust him the way you want him to trust you.

There is some other explanation for what you're seeing.

Swallowing, Sarah came forward to stand in the doorway to Scott's office, discreetly clearing her throat so that they knew someone was there.

Scott glanced up over Cleo's shaking shoulder, startled to see Sarah standing in the doorway. She'd said she was going to drop by at lunchtime so that they could go shopping together, but it was hardly that yet. He froze inside, aware that what she was seeing would not look good. No wife would be happy to find her husband with his arms wrapped around his weeping PA. Sarah wouldn't be a typical woman if she didn't jump to the wrong conclusion.

But if she did, then everything they'd achieved over the weekend would be ruined.

A fierce dismay was enveloping Scott when something wonderful happened. Sarah smiled at him, lifting her eyebrows in a way that betrayed irony rather than jealousy. She'd trusted him. Dear God, but it was an incredible feeling, bringing a lightness to his suddenly heavy soul that seemed almost miraculous.

He smiled back, lifting his shoulders in a light shrug, suggesting that he was the innocent victim of circumstance here, not some dastardly bounder.

Relief claimed Sarah when he smiled back at her, not a smidgeon of guilt in his face. Thank God she'd trusted him and not fallen into that self-destructive trap of jealousy and false assumptions.

'Hi there, darling,' he said ruefully. 'Cleo's having a bad day.'

'Oh, God, Sarah!' the woman herself cried, wrenching away from Scott's arms as if she'd been struck by lightning. 'It's not… You mustn't think… Oh, God…'

'I don't think anything,' Sarah immediately reassured her. 'Honestly.' Coming closer, she reached over to the box of tissues that Scott kept on his desk, pulled out a great wad and handed it to the still-sobbing woman.

'It's the anniversary of Martin's death,' Scott explained as Cleo mopped up her face. 'But she forgot. Till just a minute or two ago.'

'I see,' Sarah said gently.

'I've never forgotten before,' Cleo wailed, sniffling into the tissues, confusion in her voice. 'I always put flowers on his grave on the anniversary of his death,' Cleo choked out. 'I usually take his mother with me.'

'No reason why you can't still do that,' Scott said. 'Go ring Doreen now, and take the rest of the day off.'

Cleo immediately brightened. 'Are you sure?'

'Positive,' Scott said firmly.

'You are so good to me. Your husband is a wonderful man, Sarah. And a wonderful boss.'

Sarah just smiled, still slightly rattled by her initial reaction to seeing Cleo in Scott's arms. For a terrible moment there she'd let distrust raise its ugly head once more. Still, at least she hadn't let it take root. But it had been a close call.

'He certainly is,' she agreed, and linked arms with Scott.

'Off you go,' Scott told Cleo.

'Yes—yes. Right. I'm off. See you tomorrow, then, Scott. I'll just tidy up my desk and shut down my computer.'

Sarah was glad when Cleo closed the door on her way out.

'So, *madame*,' Scott said as he turned her to face him, at the same time flicking her a questioning glance. 'Are you early for lunch or did I lose track of time again?'

'I am early,' she told him smugly. 'I'm also unemployed. I resigned this morning. And I refused to work out my notice.'

Scott's eyebrows almost hit the ceiling with surprise. Sarah noted, however, that behind the surprise lay a heap of satisfaction.

'What happened? No, don't tell me, Leighton hit on you and you lost your cool.'

'Not at all,' Sarah said, having resolved during the walk over to his building not to tell Scott about her confrontation with Phil. No way did she want him charging over there and threatening to kill Phil again. So she sidestepped that part and went straight to the reasons she'd given the big boss for her rather abrupt resignation.

'From the moment I sat down at my desk this

morning,' she began, 'I knew that Goldstein & Evans wasn't the sort of place I wanted to work in either during my pregnancy, or after I have our baby. Not because of he-who-shall-not-be-named, but because it just doesn't have a parent-friendly atmosphere. Being a mother has to be my priority from now on, Scott. Being a crusading lawyer will just have to play second fiddle till our children are well on the way to growing up. Not that I intend to give up my career, mind. I might apply for a job at Legal Aid, part-time. They do very good work and it's not as though I need to earn a six-figure salary. Or do I?' she asked with a sudden jab of worry. 'You're not on the verge of bankruptcy, are you?'

Scott laughed. 'Not just yet. God, but you've no idea how happy you've just made me. But what reason did you give for resigning? And how on earth did you get away with not working out your notice?'

Sarah grinned. 'I confess that I told a few little white lies. Though there was some truth in what I said.' And there was. 'I explained that I was pregnant, though I did let Mr Goldstein think I was a little further along than I actually am. I admitted that I didn't have a sinus infection the previous week but had been suffering from shocking morning sickness. I just hadn't wanted anyone to know I was pregnant just yet. I also said my doctor had advised me to give up work for a while but I'd stubbornly refused. He accepted my resignation straight away and I came here to see you.'

'You are a seriously naughty girl,' he said, laughter in his eyes. 'But a seriously brilliant one as well.'

'True. Would you like to kiss me now?'

* * *

Scott would have liked to do more than kiss her. But Scott knew that Cleo was probably still in the outer office, tidying up and collecting her things. So he settled for just a kiss, after which he suggested they go have coffee then do some shopping.

'So what are we shopping for?' Sarah asked.

'Your anniversary present. I was going to return your idea and buy you a lovely eternity ring. And I probably will still do that. But now that you've quit your job I've decided on an added gift.'

'Oh? What?'

'A second honeymoon,' he announced.

Scott loved the joy that filled Sarah's face.

'I know how much you like Asia,' he went on, 'so I was thinking of a stay at one of the luxury beach resorts in Thailand. What about Phuket? I saw an ad for this fabulous resort there during the long week you were away, when I had to resort to watching television into the wee small hours. We could leave ASAP. What do you think?'

'Oh, I'd love it. But what about your business? Aren't things a bit sticky at the moment?'

Scott shrugged. 'Things are going to be sticky in the mining business for a long time. Our relationship is far more important than work, Sarah. We deserve some time together after what we've been through.'

'But what about this new business partner you're supposed to be getting? What about your cash-flow problems?'

'That's not so acute now that my diamond mine is producing. I have enough ready cash to keep everything afloat for at least a month or so. As for acquiring a new business partner... Cleo can handle that whilst I'm away. She knows the business inside out. She'll enjoy being the boss for a while. Besides, it's not as though we're going to be gone for all that long. Two weeks, max.'

Sarah blinked up at him. 'Heavens, I don't know what to say.'

'Just yes will do.'

Sarah shrugged. 'Okay. Yes.'

'There's a travel agency on the ground floor. We'll pop in there and see what can be arranged, post haste. But first...' He strode over, opened his office door and put his head out. 'Good, she's gone. Now...'

He returned to sweep Sarah into his arms and kiss her as he'd been aching to do. Both of them were breathing heavily by the time his head lifted.

'No,' she said when she saw that glint in his eye.

'Why not? We're married.'

Sarah had to laugh. 'What about the travel agency?'

'It's not going anywhere. Besides, this won't take long.'

'I'm not fond of quickies,' she told him even as her heartbeat accelerated.

'You could have fooled me.'

It was a glowing Sarah who sat next to Scott in the travel agency, saying yes to absolutely everything he suggested. Her arm was hooked through his and she simply couldn't stop smiling. Life was just so good. Not only did Scott love her to death but she was having his baby. Or babies. Going on a second honeymoon together would be the icing on their cake of happiness. It didn't really matter where they went. She would still enjoy it.

'So what do you say, darling?' he asked her for the umpteenth time.

She couldn't for the life of her remember what his question was about. Still, she trusted him to choose well. After all, she'd already trusted him with her life.

'Absolutely yes,' she said. 'It all sounds wonderful.'

'Are you quite sure you can be packed by tomorrow?' Scott asked her after they'd left the travel agency.

'*Tomorrow!*' Sarah exclaimed, gasping and grinding to a halt.

Scott grinned. 'I knew you weren't listening properly. But you said yes so it's a done deal. We fly out for Bangkok at four tomorrow afternoon. Think you can be ready in time?'

Sarah sucked in sharply. 'I guess I'll have to be. Oh, Lord, I have no idea what clothes to pack.'

'Not too much. We're going on a second honeymoon, remember? Clothes will not be a priority.'

'Spoken like a man. I will still need something for every possible occasion.'

Scott rolled his eyes. 'There are shops over there, you know. We can always buy whatever you might forget. Along with that eternity ring I was going to buy you today, but which we now don't have time for.'

'We certainly don't,' she said. 'I have to get home and start packing. And I'll have to go to the hairdresser in the morning. Oh, Lord!'

'They do have hairdressers over there as well,' he pointed out with a wry smile.

'True,' she agreed, all anxiety leaving her as she lifted sparkling eyes to the man she loved. 'Gosh. Tomorrow! Oh, I can hardly wait.'

Scott pulled her close. 'Neither can I, my darling. Neither can I.'

* * * * *

If you enjoyed
THE MAGNATE'S TEMPESTUOUS MARRIAGE
why not explore these other fabulous
Miranda Lee stories?

THE ITALIAN'S RUTHLESS SEDUCTION
THE BILLIONAIRE'S RUTHLESS AFFAIR
THE PLAYBOY'S RUTHLESS PURSUIT
TAKEN OVER BY THE BILLIONAIRE
A MAN WITHOUT MERCY

Available now!

AUTHOR NOTE

I WOULD NORMALLY write an epilogue to this story, but this is Book One of a series and I do not want to pre-empt anything that happens in Book Two, which will be Cleo's story.

I will not, however, leave you in suspense over the baby issue. Sarah is having twins. Not identical. A boy and a girl.

MILLS & BOON®

MODERN™

POWER, PASSION AND IRRESISTIBLE TEMPTATION

0517/01

MILLS & BOON®

EXCLUSIVE EXTRACT

Ruthless Prince Adam Katsaros offers Belle a deal –
he'll release her father if she becomes his mistress!
Adam's gaze awakens a heated desire in Belle.
Her innocent beauty might redeem his royal
reputation – but can she tame the beast inside…

Read on for a sneak preview of
THE PRINCE'S CAPTIVE VIRGIN

"You really are kind of a beast," Belle said, standing up.
Adam caught her wrist, stopped her from leaving.

"And what bothers you most about that? The fact that
you would like to reform me, that you would like for your
time here to mean something and you are beginning to see
that it won't? Or is it the fact that you don't want to reform
me at all, and that you rather like me this way. Or at least,
your body likes me this way."

"Bodies make stupid decisions all the time. My father
wanted my mother, and she was a terrible, unloving person
who didn't even want her own daughter. So, forgive me if
I find this argument rather uncompelling. It doesn't make
you a good person, just because I enjoy kissing you. And
it doesn't make this something worth exploring."

She broke free of him and began to walk away, striding
down the hall, back toward her room. He pushed away
from the table, letting his chair fall to the floor, not caring
enough to right it as he followed after Belle.

He caught up to her, pivoting so that he was in front of
her. She took a step backward, then to the side, butting up
against the wall. Then, he caged her between his arms,

staring down at her. Her blue eyes were glittering, her breasts rising and falling rapidly with each breath.

"This is the only thing worth exploring. Not what could be, but what you have. The fire that burns between you and another person. For all you know, in the days since you've been here the entire world has fallen away. And if we were all that was left… Would you not regret missing out on the chance to see how hot we could burn?"

She shook her head. "But the world hasn't fallen away," she said, her trembling lips pale now, a complete contrast to the rich color they had been only moments ago. "It's still there. And whatever happens in here will have consequences out there. I will help you, Adam, but I'm not going to give you my body. I'm not going to destroy that life that I have out there to play games with you in here. You're a stranger to me, and you're going to remain a stranger to me. I can pretend. I can give you whatever you need when it comes to making a statement for your country. But beyond that? I can't."

Then, she turned and walked away, and this time, he let her go.

Don't miss
THE PRINCE'S CAPTIVE VIRGIN
by Maisey Yates

The first part in her
ONCE UPON A SEDUCTION *trilogy*

Available June 2017
www.millsandboon.co.uk

Join Britain's BIGGEST Romance Book Club

50% OFF your first parcel

- **EXCLUSIVE offers every month**
- **FREE delivery direct to your door**
- **NEVER MISS a title**
- **EARN Bonus Book points**

Call Customer Services
0844 844 1358 *

or visit
illsandboon.co.uk/subscriptions

* This call will cost you 7 pence per minute plus your phone company's price per minute access charge.

MILLS & BOON®
are delighted to support World Book Night

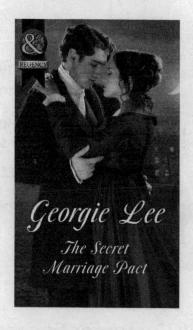

Georgie Lee

The Secret Marriage Pact